I0817814

# Southern Charm

A MAX PORTER PARANORMAL MYSTERY

Stuart Jaffe

*Southern Charm* is a work of fiction. Names, characters, places, and incidents either are the product of the author's imagination or are used fictitiously, and any resemblance to any persons, living or dead, business establishments, events, or locales is entirely coincidental.

SOUTHERN CHARM



Cover art by Duncan Long

ISBN 13: 978-1-7337308-4-6

First Edition: June, 2012
Second Edition: May, 2014
First Hardcover Edition: December, 2023

For Dave, Val, and Vaughn

# Also by Stuart Jaffe

*Max Porter Paranormal Mysteries*

- Southern Bound
- Southern Charm
- Southern Belle
- Southern Gothic
- Southern Haunts
- Southern Curses
- Southern Rites
- Southern Craft
- Southern Spirit
- Southern Flames
- Southern Fury
- Southern Souls
- Southern Blood
- Southern Graves
- Southern Dead
- Southern Hexes
- Southern Hart

*Nathan K Thrillers*

- Immortal Killers
- Killing Machine
- The Cardinal
- Yukon Massacre
- The First Battle
- Immortal Darkness
- A Spy for Eternity
- Prisoner
- Desert Takedown
- Lone Star Standoff
- The Puppeteer
- Blowback
- Prime

*The Ridnight Mysteries*

- The Water Blade
- The Waters of Taladoro
- Waterfire

*The Parallel Society*

The Infinity Caverns
Book on the Isle
Rift Angel
Lost Time
Pages of Glass
The Bold Warrior
City of Infinity

*The Malja Chronicles*

The Way of the Black Beast
The Way of the Sword and Gun
The Way of the Brother Gods
The Way of the Blade
The Way of the Power
The Way of the Soul

*Gillian Boone novels*

A Glimpse of Her Soul
Pathway to Spirit

*Stand Alone Novels*

After The Crash
Real Magic
Founders

*Short Story Collection*

10 Bits of My Brain
10 More Bits of My Brain
The Bluesman
The Marshall Drummond Case Files: Cabinet 1
The Marshall Drummond Case Files: Cabinet 2
The Marshall Drummond Case Files: Cabinet 3

*Non-Fiction*

How to Write Magical Words: A Writer's Companion
For more information, please visit ***www.stuartjaffe.com***

# Acknowledgments

All books require more than just the author's work, and this book is no different. This time around, my thanks go out to the helpful and indulgent people at Korner's Folly; Duncan Long, for another fantastic cover; my good friend and honest reader, Garrett; all of my family for their constant support; and my closest and dearest, Glory and Gabe. And of course, none of my jabbering amounts to anything without somebody to read it. So to you, the reader, thank you.

# Southern Charm

# Chapter 1

MAX PORTER STARED AT THE RED NUMBER on his computer screen. It taunted him like a tiny, red devil daring him to quit, daring him to run away. His stomach gurgled in discomfort. "It's not fair," he said.

Sandra, his wife, glanced up from her desk. "What's that?"

The office was small, so he knew she had heard him. Just another example of how things had gone wrong. When they had first moved to North Carolina, she worked in a bakery, and though they struggled, they managed to get by — enjoying each other in the process. Since she had joined in the office, though, tension surrounded him. He could never just go home. Work always followed.

Pointing at the devilish number, he said, "I've been so careful, but we're still losing money. It's crazy. Heck, we don't even have to pay rent on this place, and we're still in the red."

Max could feel his frustration rising and tried to hide it. Sandra had been after him lately not to let every unsettling detail rip into him, but being self-employed came with a lot of unsettling details — the health insurance costs alone could send him to a hospital he couldn't afford. Though she didn't say a word, he could feel her thoughts as if they were jagged rocks pressing into his neck.

He rose from behind his huge oak desk and headed toward the office bookcase — a gorgeous built-in case filled with books on the area, its history, as well as a few on witchcraft and other oddities. A bottle of whiskey had been hidden in one of the books, and Max thought a little numbing might be in order. Before he could locate the book, though, Drummond stuck his head through the wall.

"It's a bit early in the morning for that," he said. The ghost slid further into the office, wearing the suit he had died in during the 1940s. Marshall Drummond was tall, well-built, and handsome, but since the office once had belonged to him, his in-house manners were less desirable.

"Good morning, Marshall," Sandra said.

"Morning, Sugar."

Max detoured from the bookshelf and gazed out the window. Though early fog covered Winston-Salem, he could still make out the old YMCA across the street. The office was only three stories up, yet the people heading to work looked small and humble.

"Sometimes," Max said, sitting back in his leather chair and rubbing his face, "I hate to admit it, but I actually think working for Hull hadn't been so bad."

Sandra glanced at Max with her eyebrow raised. "Sure, it was wonderful. Lots of fun and smiles every day — except for the way they threatened us, beat and kidnapped you, and then had their witch try to curse you."

"Yeah, other than that. Really the money's what I miss."

"Patience, honey. It takes a lot to get a business going, and this isn't the kind you can effectively advertise for. It's all word of mouth for us."

Drummond clapped his hands together making a singular, firm noise, and pointed to Sandra. "You listen to her. That gal of yours knows what she's saying. She's got a good head on her shoulders. Beautiful, charming head at that."

"Not interested," Sandra said as Drummond playfully scowled.

Max wished he could be as light-hearted as they were. None of these troubles seemed to bother them. Drummond was right about one thing though — Sandra looked extra beautiful that morning. Shaking his head to refocus, he said, "The problem is nobody knows what to make of us. We're not a detective agency, we're not a research firm doing polls — we're just researchers."

Sandra frowned. "Don't say it like that. You're gifted at this. You find things nobody else can."

"Everybody can. I'm just willing to put in the work."

"Well, that's why people hire us. They don't want to put in the work. And this kind of in-depth research requires waiting for word to get out about us. And look here —" Sandra said, pointing to the empty client chair.

"I know, I know. Let's get back to work. Fill that chair."

"No, Max, I —"

Max raised a hand, his eyes on the accounting program on his screen, the income/expense graphs, the blazing red number, and let out a long sigh. "It's the ghosts," he said.

Drummond perked up. "You're going to blame me?"

"Not you. The clients."

Sandra tried to shush him with her hands. "I don't think you—"

"I don't care if Drummond gets all ruffled. The fact is that we're the only investigative body that will deal with ghosts. Heck, we're probably the only ones that can even see them, and yet they don't really pay, do they? I mean, gratitude only goes so far."

Drummond slid forward, snatching a peek at the client chair. "It's more interesting than looking up somebody's genealogy."

"At least that pays."

Sandra glared at Drummond. "Honey, stop —"

Max's mouth tightened. "You're going to take his side?"

"I'm not taking his side."

Drummond stepped behind her with a sly wink. "Sure she is. The kid knows when I'm right, and I'm rarely wrong."

"You know what?" Max said. "I don't care. This is my business. These are my bills. My name is on it all. So from now on, no ghosts unless they prove to us they can pay."

Crossing her arms, Sandra said, "You are making —"

"Biggest mistake of my life, I know. But, honey, you're not seeing the numbers. You're not the one fretting over the mortgage on our house. And I do understand that you like the ghosts. I mean, for me, I just see Drummond and that's it — which ain't always a picnic. But you've been seeing them your whole life. You see them everywhere. You have a different perspective and all that. A different relationship with all of it. I do understand. But you've got to understand that I'm not going back to the way things were in Michigan. I won't do it. I don't want us to be that desperate for money ever again. Okay? So that's that. No more ghosts unless the damn things pay."

"Are you finished?" Sandra asked in a calm tone that worried Max.

"Um ... yeah."

"Good. Because I've been trying to tell you that there's another ghost sitting in our client chair."

"Oh." Max pushed out a grin toward the empty chair and tried to ignore Drummond's stifled giggles. "Hi, there."

Drummond walked next to the chair and said, "This is Max Porter. Max, meet Howard Corkille, our new client."

# Chapter 2

FROM HIS DESK, Max pulled out a notebook and a pen. Despite the previous outburst, he managed a somewhat responsible pose and said, "I apologize for what you heard."

"He says, 'It's okay.' He understands the pressures you face and wants you to know that he can and will pay for your services," Drummond said, settling on the edge of Max's desk. "Besides, Corkille here has nowhere else to go."

"Perhaps we shouldn't insult the client anymore than we already have today."

"All I'm saying is that we ghosts sometimes have limited choices, and Howard here understands that."

Max held back from further comment. Experience had taught him that to say anything would only provoke Drummond further. Instead, he looked straight at the empty chair and said, "Mr. Corkille, I'm afraid I can't see or hear you. Apparently, I'm only tuned in to Mr. Drummond. My wife, however, can see and hear you just fine. She can act as our interpreter, if that's okay with you."

Sandra smiled at Corkille, listened, and then repeated his words for Max. "'There are ways for you to see me. I could reach into you and —'"

"Experiencing that once was enough for a lifetime," Max said. He'd never forget the icy pain he had endured at the Old Salem cemetery when a ghost reached into his head. "Besides, the pain is so severe that I wouldn't be able to listen clearly to anything you say. Trust us. This is the best way to handle this."

Sandra touched the back of the client chair. "It's okay. You can talk with us."

"Did you forget why you're here?" Drummond said. "You asked me to help you out. I brought you to the guy that'll do it.

Now out with your story."

Intending to ease over Drummond's harsh approach, Max pushed back in his chair, but Sandra repeated for Corkille, "'Wait. I'm sorry. Please, don't get up. I'm just a little nervous.'"

Max played along and pulled closer. "What can we do for you?"

"Slow down, Mr. Corkille," Sandra said. Then after a moment, she continued. "'It's all about my granddaughter. Well, her and a painting. I am ... I was ... an artist. My specialty was in replicating the styles of well-known personages and providing those newer artworks to museums and collectors.'"

Drummond laughed. "He's an art forger."

"'Don't be so dismissive. It takes training, skill, and knowledge to successfully mimic the great artists. In many ways, it's more difficult than what the Masters have accomplished themselves.'"

Max pretended to write in his notebook, a touch he'd picked up over the last year — clients liked to believe that every detail was deemed important. "Go on," he said.

"'Yes, well, you see, back in 1930 things were very difficult for me and my wife. The Depression hit us early on. Others we knew managed to survive for another year or so, but we didn't have much to begin with. Before, I had been doing artwork for advertising and such, you see, but the Crash ruined the company I worked for — the owner had been borrowing money to buy equipment but instead invested it in the stock market. One day, they just closed up. After that, I couldn't get work. I tried, but nobody wanted to hire me. And then my darling wife got pregnant.

"'I panicked. I do that. I don't handle that kind of pressure too well. That is, I didn't. I put out the word that I was an artist for hire. I tried everywhere. Mostly, I just got laughed at. I'm not a big man.' He wants me to tell you what I see."

"Okay."

Sandra pointed to parts of the empty chair as she spoke. "He's thin, probably was a bit lanky when he was alive. He's got a mustache ... what? ... he says that he only grew the mustache a few months before he died. Thick glasses, bony fingers." She chuckled. "I'm sorry, Mr. Corkille, I'm just doing what you asked."

Max bristled but wrote down the description. "If you're done flirting with my wife, can we continue?"

A comforting gaze from Sandra relaxed Max a bit. Then she said, "He apologizes. He says, 'The point is that I could never do any of the hard labor that was left to most men. Even if I could've done the work, the brutal fights just to get the jobs — I had heard enough to know that was not the route for me.

"'I was ready to give up. You see, I even stole a steak and traded it for a small handgun. I planned to kill myself and let what little money I had help Clara, that's my wife, but that was not meant to be the way of things.

"'The day I chose to do it — I can see it so clearly — I went out into the tobacco fields and had my gun and I had drunk a bottle of cheap wine to prepare myself. But then a man I had never seen before grabbed the gun from my hand.

"'I asked him what he thought he was doing. I really yelled at him, and I remember thinking how drunk I must be to speak so boldly.

"'He introduced himself — I don't see that his name is important to this, so I'll just call him Mr. Smith.'"

Max put his pen down, making sure the action created a sharp snap. "It's best if you let us decide which details are important and which are not."

"'Oh, I understand that, I do. But you see, in this case, the man has been dead longer than me, so you cannot possibly —'"

"I can't force you, but just know that any details you omit will only make our job harder."

"'Well, Mr. Smith,'" Sandra said, and Max imagined Corkille straightening his back and jutting out his chin, "'asked me if I was the artist looking for work. I was astonished, of course, and I told him so. He said that he'd been looking for me for some time, checking out as much as he could on me, because he had a sensitive job he needed my skills for.

"'I had done some forgeries before but mostly for my own amusement and study. It never occurred to me to try to make serious money off of it. I feared jail too much. But my wife was expecting, we had no money, and by this time my resolve toward suicide had gone away. Mr. Smith wanted me to forge a specific painting, make an exact replica, for which he would pay me five hundred dollars. That was an enormous sum back then. I just couldn't turn that kind of opportunity away. I had to take it.'"

"I understand completely," Max said.

"'I suppose you do. So, I did the painting. It wasn't a famous work. It wasn't a famous artist. Just a landscape, really, with a slight nod toward Monet. He called it "Morning in Red" except it had little red in it. When I was done, Mr. Smith paid me and asked me to hold on to the painting for a few days while he made certain arrangements.'"

Drummond rested his hands on his knees and said, "Never saw the guy again, did you?"

"'No, but I read in the papers he was killed in an accident.'"

"What did you do with the painting?"

"'I held on to it. A few years later, I died. Slipped in front of an oncoming train. Didn't even know I was dead for quite some time. Never got to see my son grow up, let alone the birth of my granddaughter.'"

Max said, "It's an intriguing tale. What exactly do you want to hire us for?"

"'You see, my granddaughter — I've never seen her.'"

"So you want us to find her?"

"'Yes.'"

"What's her name?"

"'Melinda. I don't know if she ever married.'"

"And you think she's here in Winston-Salem?"

"'I don't know, but, you see, we've always lived in this area or nearby. I can't imagine she would go too far. Even if she did, we were always here.'"

"Drummond, write down Howard's address when he lived here."

Drummond scowled — it was painful for a ghost to interact so directly with the corporeal world — but Max wanted Sandra focusing on Corkille. As Drummond wrote, Sandra continued, "'Before you find her, though, first, I want you to find the painting. I've met many unique ghosts in the past decades, one of which was an art collector. We've had some great talks. When I told him my story, he said that some collectors specialized in forgeries and would love to have a piece with such a colorful tale associated with it. You see, I believe that painting could be auctioned today for substantial money. So, I want you to find it and then find Melinda. You may split the proceeds evenly between you and her. I believe that should cover your bill whatever it ends up being. But I want her to have some money. I couldn't be there for her father or her, at least I can do this. And, well, I suppose that's my story. Will you help me?'"

Before Max could speak, Drummond blurted out, "Of course, we'll help you. That's what we do. You just let us do our thing and don't worry at all ... you're very welcome. I'll let you know when we've found the painting ... yes, yes, and you're granddaughter. Don't worry."

Sandra looked up from the client chair. "He's gone."

Too tired from arguing over money, Max didn't bother laying into Drummond. Besides, maybe this painting would actually be worth something. "Okay, let's get organized," Max said, and Drummond's shock made his restraint worthwhile. "Sandra, I want you to check out Howard Corkille. If his family has been here as much as he's implied, there should be plenty of records to find. Drummond, you and I are going to visit that address."

"What about the painting?" Drummond asked.

Max shook his head. "All we have is a name, and Corkille said that the painting isn't famous or by anybody well-known. I doubt it was ever exhibited."

"But the client wants that done first, and that painting is the income source for this job. Besides, there's an art gallery just below us. We can start there and then go to the address."

"Fine, but there's no need to go downstairs. We can search for the painting online. That's what search engines are for."

"In case you forgot, I'm dead. I get to see computers, not use them. I still don't quite get it all, but then again, learning the thing's not been a pressing need. Look, I'm not trying to tell you how to research stuff. I'm just an old detective. When we get to the crimes, I'll know what to do."

"There's no crime in this."

"Art forgery's a crime."

"We're just finding an old painting and a granddaughter," Max said, but he didn't doubt Drummond's cold expression — this was going to get complicated.

A few mouse clicks, a few keystrokes, and Max knew he would not be finding "Morning in Red" online. No surprise, though. The painting pre-dated the computer age, and it's obscurity made it doubtful anybody would bother scanning and uploading the image.

Max tried a few other avenues, but nothing turned up. He didn't want to listen to Drummond's gloating, but the case came first. Grabbing his coat, he said, "Come on. We need to see that art gallery downstairs."

"Oh, really," Drummond said, but Max already had reached the stairwell.

# Chapter 3

DEACON ARTS OCCUPIED the first floor of the building. The remaining floors were mostly apartments and Max's office, all of which had been built in the 1930s. This first floor space, however, sported a more modern look — and at first glance, more modern amenities as well.

Like most galleries, this one adhered to an open, flowing layout, with well-lit paintings on the walls and curving sculptures in the middle. An antique desk faced out from the back corner, a computer resting on its edge, and behind it sat a heavy-set man, balding with a white goatee. Flashing an elitist smile, he said, "Good morning." His voice flowed with a smooth drawl that Max had become accustomed to hearing after a year in the South.

"Morning," Max said, looking around the room. The paintings varied in style and color — no specific theme tied any of it together. Drummond floated from one work to the next, his face pressing in close to each painting.

"May I help you?"

Max glanced at the desk's nameplate. "Mr. Gold?"

"That is my name."

"I was wondering if you could help me locate a specific painting that I'm trying to find."

Without looking, Drummond said, "Don't be so wordy. Makes you seem untrustworthy."

Mr. Gold gestured to a seat near his desk and posed his fingers over the computer keyboard. "Let's see what we can do. What's the name of the painting and the artist?"

"The painting is 'Morning in Red' and the artist —"

Mr. Gold did not type. For an instant, Max thought the man might be having a heart attack. Then Mr. Gold said with forced casualness, "'Morning in Red' — I've never heard of it."

"It's not a famous work."

"Well, I'll try online but —"

"I've already tried the public search engines. Mostly get hits on the old, 'Red skies at night, sailor's delight. Red skies at morning, sailor take warning.' You, however, should have access to some kind of art gallery database."

"Naturally, I do, but I can't really abuse that privilege on every request, particularly for such an unknown artwork. Besides, searches on that database cost us money. So, you see, I can't just —"

Pulling out his wallet, Max said, "I'd be happy to cover the cost." Not *happy,* really. He only had three dollars.

"It's not that simple," Mr. Gold said, fumbling with two books and piling them on the floor. "I have to get permissions."

Drummond slid behind him and looked at the books. "This guy's lying. You know that, right?"

Max nodded.

"Good," Drummond went on, "because these books he tried to hide are all about art forgery." Sometimes Max loved having a ghost for partner.

Seizing onto an idea, Mr. Gold said, "Let me take down your name and number, and I'll see what I can learn for you. We're just at the beginning of the day. I'm sure I can —"

"The painting is 'Morning in Red.' My name's Max Porter and my office is right upstairs — 319."

"Of course. I thought I'd recognized you. I see you walk in many mornings."

"Let us know when you find something."

"Us?"

"My wife works up there as well."

"Ah, yes, I see. Well, Mr. Porter, I'll do my best, but I wouldn't expect much. A little painting like that, one that has probably never been shown in a gallery or sold in such, that is most likely not in anybody's database."

"You just give it a try."

Though Mr. Gold prattled on with excuses and concerns, Max never looked back as he left the gallery. Drummond circled his partner with excited swoops. "That's the way you should always do this. You're finally learning. Wonderful. That liar wasn't going to help us out anyway. Might as well give him a hard time."

As Max climbed the stairs to his office, he said, "Don't you think it's weird that Gold is lying about the painting? I mean, we just got the case. Nobody could know we were hired, let alone what we were looking for."

"This is the detective racket," Drummond said. "Just because you can't legally call yourself that, doesn't mean you aren't one. And let me tell you something I want you to remember always. By the time somebody's knocking on your door, by the time they've finally admitted they need you, there are already many others involved."

"So somebody else is looking for this painting."

"More than one somebody, most likely."

"Mr. Porter! Mr. Porter!" Mr. Gold shouted from downstairs. With labored breaths and one arm gripping the railings as if he might fall over at any moment, Mr. Gold reached the third floor.

Not hiding his amusement, Drummond passed through Mr. Gold several times, causing the sweating man to shiver. "Seems to be a draft up here."

"Yeah," Max said. "That happens sometimes. What is it?"

"Here," Mr. Gold said, handing over a paper. "I decided to do a public search — I know you said you did one, but it all depends on what keywords you use and how you put them in. I thought I might have better luck since I do this kind of searching all the time. Anyway, I found your painting and that's the address. So, good luck with that and I'll be going now."

Moving faster than he had arrived, Mr. Gold scurried down the stairs. Drummond watched with disdain. "Well, that wasn't the least bit suspicious."

Max snickered. "Yeah."

Mrs. Amos shuffled out of her apartment to pick up the

morning paper at her door, squinted at Max talking to himself, scowled, and closed the door. The old woman never had much more for Max. The most he had ever gotten from her was a "Go to Hell" when he called her by name (a tidbit he acquired from her mailbox). The shock on her face still made him smile.

"You know," Drummond said as he passed through the closed office door, "I like that old gal."

When Max entered the office, Sandra kissed him and asked, "How'd it go?"

"We got an address," Max said, reading the paper for the first time. "Some place west in Clemmons. Probably nothing useful, though."

"I did better than that," she said like a schoolyard tease.

"I'm listening."

"Me, too," Drummond said from his usual perch in the bookcase.

Sandra held out a piece of paper like a winning lottery ticket. "That is the address of one Melinda Corkille. I started checking out the family name when it occurred to me to 4-1-1 her name first. She lives just south of here in Davidson County."

Max frowned.

"What's wrong?" she asked.

"This address. It's the same one Corkille gave us. The one in which he last lived."

Drummond perked up. "Really? Why would he not know where she was living then?"

"That's what I'm wondering."

"Especially after our art gallery visit. You know, I hate to say it, but this whole thing smells real bad."

"Thanks for the input. Why don't you go find your ghost friend and get us some real information? Sandra, find out what you can on Corkille, this house, and anything on that painting. I'm going to visit Melinda Corkille."

# Chapter 4

AS HE DROVE DOWN Peters Creek Parkway toward Davidson County, Max tried to blot out any guilt he felt toward Sandra. He knew she would be mad at him later, but for now he had to focus. Except why should he be feeling this way at all? He could tell by how her body drooped when he gave out their assignments that she had expected to accompany him to Melinda Corkille's house — but angry? Why should she be angry?

"Don't act so innocent," Max said to the empty car. He knew from the start that she would want to come along. If for no other reason, it beat the heck out of sitting in the office working on a computer. But he couldn't bring her. He needed some space.

"That's really it, isn't it?" The past year had been hard on them in a way like never before. Always in the office together, always at home together, in the car together — he loved her, deep to his bones love, but she smothered him with her constant presence.

He wanted her to go back to the bakery. She would bring in some money for them while he struggled to get his business off the ground. Most important, she would be happy, independent, and not pissed because Max had to be the boss.

"Only one problem, though, Max." One enormous problem. Sandra could see the ghosts. How could he run his business without that special skill? Of course, he could just go the route everybody else did, but Drummond was right about that — he hated researching one boring genealogy after another. Those just paid the bills, and they often didn't do that much. These types of cases — the ones that were otherworldly — these were the things that gave him that investigative rush.

And for that to continue, he needed Sandra.

*What about Drummond?* He laughed at the thought. He liked Drummond — sometimes — and he did respect the man's talents as a private investigator, but he could never trust the man the way he trusted Sandra.

As he neared the county line, the landscape became a typical suburban sprawl — wide, open land being cultivated into megastores, parking lots, housing developments, and twelve-pump gas station/convenience stores. Widening roads and erecting new streetlights added to the hubbub, slowing traffic and littering the pavement with North Carolina's famous red clay. *In a few more years, Winston-Salem will engulf this all.*

Davidson County proved to be more of a traditional suburban landscape and even a bit rural. It all had been farm land once, but the modern world left its mark. Though it did not bear the industrial charms of Winston-Salem, neither did it cleave to a pristine beauty that is often written about in the history books. Max knew from years of reading such things that the history books lied — the old days were never pristine and beautiful. Still, he wondered if, when compared to today's cities, some rolling farmland might not be such a bad thing.

The Corkille home sat in the middle of several well-tended acres. Though a large place, Max did not consider it a mansion — just a big house. It reminded him of a 19th century estate that grew as the family grew. Then, throughout the 20th century, acre after acre was sold off until all that remained was the house itself and enough acreage to remind the family of what once was.

He pulled up the horseshoe driveway, wheels on gravel crunching his arrival, and stopped at the front door. A young woman stepped out wearing an outfit meant to look casual despite a price tag that would have paid Max's heating bill for several years. She cradled a coffee mug and shrugged her blond ponytail off her shoulder. More than anything, however, Max's attention ignited at the sight of her lips — thick, seductive lips that curved into a welcoming smile strong enough to jump up Max's heart rate.

As he got out of his car, he could only think how fortunate that Drummond had not come along. The comments alone would have driven Max nuts.

"Good morning. I'm Max Porter."

"Good morning. Melinda Corkille. What can I do for you?"

Max chuckled. "You're very friendly. Most people would be a lot more cautious when a stranger pulls up to their door. Especially one in a beat up Honda that probably sounds as bad as it looks."

Melinda sipped her coffee and smiled again. "I'm a firm believer that the world is not much worse than it ever was. It's just that we hear about everything the moment it happens."

"That doesn't mean bad things don't happen."

"No, but it does mean that being friendly to you is just as safe as it was ten years ago."

Max put out his hand. "Since that benefits me, I won't argue anymore. I'm Max Porter."

"You said that already."

"Indeed, I did," Max said with a goofy bow. "You have a beautiful home, by the way."

Blushing, Melinda said, "Okay, Mr. Porter, you've made some nice small talk and you're complimenting my home. What's this all about?"

"I'm writing a book on art forgery —"

"And the name Howard Corkille came up, did it?"

"Yes, it did."

"And you just thought you could come by here unannounced with a smile and some charm and what? I'd just hand everything over to you?"

"No," Max said, opening his hands in a friendly gesture, "not quite like that. Really, I only found out about him this morning and I came down in my excitement. I'm sorry. I should've called first."

"Yes, you should've. Where are you from, Mr. Porter? You sound Northern."

"Guilty," he said with a chuckle, but Melinda did not smile. "I'm from Michigan most recently, but I've lived in Winston-

Salem for over a year now. I love it here. I don't ever want to leave."

"Pity," she said and turned back to her house.

"Wait, please. I don't want to hurt your family or your name or disrespect you in any way. I simply want to look into how and why an art forger does what he does. Maybe find some of his work."

Standing in her doorway, Melinda said, "None of his work is left. It was all destroyed years ago in a fire."

Max frowned. "I didn't know that."

"Now you do."

"A fire. Was it here?"

Pointing with her coffee mug, she said, "Took the entire East wing to the ground. Became big news for awhile and made things hard around here. It was pretty ugly, I'm told."

"Still, there must be some of his work around. Work that wasn't in the house."

With a playful push, Melinda said, "Aren't you cute, trying to dance around a question."

"I only meant —"

"I know what you meant. You want to know about the works he passed off onto others. But, now, you said you didn't want to cause us any trouble or embarrassment. Isn't that right?"

"Yes, of course."

"If you pursue these paintings, don't you think you might cause us a little embarrassment and a lot of trouble?"

Using what he hoped played as boyish charm, he gave in and said, "I'm sorry. Sometimes my enthusiasm gets the better of me. I'm not really that interested in all of the paintings, anyway. Just one in particular. Maybe you can tell me if it survived the fire. It's called 'Morning in Red' and —"

Her gorgeous smile dropped to a tight line. "Goodbye, Mr. Porter," she said and closed the door.

Max stood still for a moment, knowing she would be watching him from some vantage point. He slouched, attempting a defeated appearance, and walked back to his car.

From the driveway, he turned right onto the main road and another right at the corner. Then he sped around the block until he came toward the house again and could park a few cars back.

*Drummond'll like this one.* He could hear the ghost in his head say, "You're finally catching on to the detective racket."

Though he had spent time waiting in a car before, nothing equaled the mixture of tension and boredom that came from a stakeout. Every car passing by, every child shouting to her friends, every protest from the driver's seat when Max shifted his weight, magnified in his ears as he anticipated Melinda. Close to an hour had passed when Max's cell phone rang.

"Hello?"

"Hi, Max. Is this a bad time?" His mother.

"Hi, Mom. I'm working right now. Can I call you back?"

"Sure, that's fine. Just make sure you really do call me back because sometimes you say you will and then you forget. Not that I mind. I'm your mother. I understand being forgotten and mothers don't hold it against their young, but I do have something important to share so —"

Melinda's tan Mercedes convertible pulled onto the road. "I'll call you back. I promise," Max said, snapped the phone shut, and followed the car.

They headed back up Peters Creek Parkway toward the city. Max wiped the sweat from his hands on his pants. Melinda drove fast, forcing Max to find an uncomfortable balance between staying close to her with not being obvious by driving as fast as she chose. She weaved around traffic, never using her turn signal, so Max had no clue where she would go next.

He ran a red light, gained the loving honks of annoyed drivers, but kept sight of the tan Mercedes. As they went downhill, she cut left across two lanes in order to get to the on-ramp for highway 40.

"Damn," he said. Traffic had boxed him in, but as he passed by Melinda, he saw her take the westbound lane.

At the next light, he made a U-turn, sped up and ran the yellow to get onto the highway. Considering how fast she drove on regular roads, he guessed she'd push around ninety on the highway. Crossing his fingers against any cops, he pressed on the gas.

At eighty, the car shuddered. At eighty-five, it whined. At ninety, it made noises Max had never heard.

Slapping the steering wheel and spitting out a few curses, Max eased back on the gas. His old car sighed as the strain released. He looked around on the dim hope he might still see her, but no sign of her car could be found.

Max took the next exit for Lewisville-Clemmons Road and pulled into a gas station. His damp collar rubbed against his neck and his hands shook. He left his car, stretched, and tried to calm his racing pulse.

It was possible that Melinda Corkille always drove that fast. And it was possible she knew Max was following her, and she successfully escaped.

Max frowned. *The Lewisville-Clemmons exit.* He rushed back to his car and found the paper Mr. Gold had given him — an address where Max supposedly would find the painting; an address in Clemmons. Before he could ask himself the question "Is it just a coincidence that Melinda Corkille headed in the direction of Clemmons?" he heard Drummond in his head — *There are no coincidences.*

# Chapter 5

FROM UNDER THE PASSENGER SEAT, Max pulled out his Winston-Salem map. Styer's Ferry Road began a few miles north and wound all around the area. He had no illusions that he would discover the painting, but he also had no idea what he might actually find — and that troubled him the most.

In just a few minutes drive, Styer's Ferry Road arrived, and within a mile, the world became rural. Sheep farms and horse farms, pine thickets and rotting houses, all littered the landscape. In front of him drove a pickup truck with several Confederate flag bumper stickers pasted to the gate. One said in proud Confederate print:

I ♥ G. R. I. T. S.
Girls Raised In The South

Max pointed from his steering wheel and grinned. He could hear his mother warning him about moving to the South. No matter how much he tried to convince her that people weren't like the stereotypes down here, she always responded, "Stereotypes exist because stereotypes exist." Looking at Mr. Grits in front of him made her point.

When he pulled in the driveway matching the address on the paper, Max considered pulling away. An unkempt yard fronted a dilapidated double-wide trailer. A brown sedan, dented and dirty, idled in the driveway.

Somebody was home.

Max got out, covered his mouth against the rank car fumes sputtering into the air, and headed up the driveway. As he passed the brown sedan, he noticed that numerous packages covered the backseat. Several more were stacked on the passenger seat, and two clipboards with US Postal Service paperwork occupied the driver's seat.

Something felt off about this place. Not just the way in which Mr. Gold had magically appeared with the address but with the place itself. Max thought of old horror movies and childhood fears — haunted house tales that left him with nightmares for over a week.

Without stopping to think it over, Max opened the car door and turned off the engine. The sudden absence of the noisy engine left only the wind rustling the leaves high above. That near silence increased Max's unsettled tension.

He glanced back at his car. He should just go. Go back to the office, tell Sandra and Drummond everything, and then come back here with them both.

He glanced at the trailer. But it was broad daylight, mid-day in fact. Nothing to be frightened of here. Besides hadn't he dealt with ghosts and witches? This was just a stupid trailer in the middle of a bright day.

It was quiet, though. Why should Mr. Gold send him to an address in which nobody was there? Except somebody had to be there. The brown sedan had been running.

"Come on, get moving," Max said, and with that he strode to the trailer's front step. He opened the screen door and knocked. "Hello?" He knocked again. "Hello?"

No answer.

He decided to do something he had seen in movies many times and always thought *Who would ever actually do that?* He turned the doorknob. To his surprise, it opened. Before he could warn himself, before he could scream inside to turn around, get in his car, and get the hell out of there, he heard a gurgling moan that chilled his heart.

With cautious steps, he entered the kitchen — a filthy, beaten room that smelled of rotten food and urine. The kitchen opened into a living room that fared no better — stained blue carpet matted and torn, thick stink of cigarettes, and in the center, a large man tied to a chair. He had been beaten. Blood trailed lines down his face, neck, and arms. His right eye had swollen and bloody spittle dribbled from his mouth. The gore still glistened on his US Postal Service uniform and covered his name, Curtis, in dark splotches.

At the sound of Max's footsteps, Curtis perked up his head, his body shaking, and said through a damaged mouth, "I swear I don't know anything about anything. I swear. I never wanted any picture. I swear. Just don't hurt me anymore."

"It's okay," Max said. "I'm not one of them."

"Then get me out of here." Curtis's voice broke into a panic. "Get me out of here before they come back. Help me! Please!"

"Calm down. I'm going to get you out."

"It wasn't me. I didn't do anything. It couldn't have been me. I was just making a delivery."

"I know," Max said, kneeling down.

"I-I ... didn't do anything. I swear."

Curtis held his breath a moment as if he couldn't process anymore without stalling other body functions. Then he exhaled and sobbed. Max stayed silent while he worked loose the blood-drenched ropes that had bound the man. What more could he say? Curtis had picked the wrong time to deliver a package. That's all. And what had been meant for Max had been done on this uninvolved man.

*But it had been meant for me.* The realization struck the depths of his stomach, threatening to reprise his breakfast. He could see the faceless attackers waiting all morning. Mr. Gold had told those blood-thirsty thugs that he had passed on the address to the target — it was only a matter of waiting. Except one of them or all of them couldn't be patient. When Curtis arrived, they decided to act. It wasn't until they started listening to their victim that they understood they had tortured the wrong person. Then they ran.

Or maybe they never figured out they had made a mistake. Whichever the case, Max knew that they had intended for his body to be covered in blood, his bones to be broken, his mouth to be swollen. This was all for him.

Curtis crumpled to the floor, still crying, clutching his ribs, and rocking like a child. Max pictured himself in that position

— the one somebody had intended for him. "I'm sorry," he said, but Curtis did not respond.

"Help is coming," Max said. On his cell, he called 9-1-1, left the address and said a man was dying, then ended the call. "Hang on. An ambulance is coming."

He couldn't wait around, though. There would be questions and a trip to the police and if Curtis didn't make it, there would be no one to back up his story. He had to go.

As Max drove away, his heart racing, the salty taste of his sweat on his lips, he kept imagining his own body curled on that disgusting floor. All over a nothing painting. "Not nothing anymore," he said. Turning onto the highway, heading back to the office, he knew there were several avenues to pursue, but one demanded immediate attention — Howard Corkille.

It took Max twenty minutes to get back to the office, and halfway there, his anger boiled up again. Blood-soaked images of Curtis flashed through his mind. He had to do something about that or somebody else might get hurt — maybe even him. By the time he parked his car, Howard Corkille had been pushed to the number two priority.

Max slammed open the door to Deacon Arts. Mr. Gold, fawning over a customer, jumped at the sound, saw Max, and let out a babyish yelp. "Mr. Porter," he said, backing up with his hands out. "I just delivered the message."

"I'm going to fucking kill you."

The customer scurried out fast, and Mr. Gold could not hide his disappointment at losing a sale. When Max moved in, Mr. Gold's disappointment turned to fear. He stumbled over himself as he rushed back to his desk. Max followed right behind, grabbed Mr. Gold's arm, yanked him around, and punched him in the eye.

Mr. Gold cried out and fell into his seat. "Please, don't. I'm sorry. I had to do it. I'm sorry."

"Where's the painting?"

"I don't know."

"Do I have to hit you again?"

"I swear I don't know," Mr. Gold said, tears and snot

flowing down his face. "I never heard of the painting. I was just told to give you that address."

"By who?"

With an incredulous frown, Mr. Gold said, "By Mr. Modesto, of course. Who would you expect?"

Breathing hard, his fist poised to strike again, Max stepped back, stunned by the name. Mr. Modesto. The Hull family representative. And if they were involved, this whole case became far more complicated.

# Chapter 6

WHEN MAX ENTERED THE OFFICE, Sandra gasped. "What happened to you?" she asked as she rushed to his side. "Are you hurt?"

Max glanced down — blood marred his shirt. "It's not mine," he said, thinking of Curtis the US Postal Service guy and his wrecked body.

Sandra helped Max to his chair. Without a word, she then pulled one of Drummond's fake books from the bookcase, grabbed the flask inside, and poured a glass of whiskey. Max drank fast, coughed, sputtered, and drank again.

"Don't you look all spiffy?" Drummond said, gliding through the front wall. "Can't say I'm surprised."

"You say anything else remotely resembling 'I told you so' and I swear, ghost or not, I'll find a way to make you sorry."

To Sandra, Drummond said, "Little touchy. What happened?"

"I don't know."

Max rubbed his sore knuckles — punching a person hurt. "What'd Corkille have to say?"

Drummond settled in the client chair and put his feet on the desk. "I couldn't find him."

"What do you mean?" Sandra said.

"Sugar, the netherworld of ghosts is larger than you'd imagine, and there's a lot of us. Of all people, I'd expect you to understand that much. So I looked, asked around, but I couldn't find him. If he wasn't already dead, I'd suspect somebody got to him."

"Don't you think it's odd that Corkille would hire us and then not be available?"

"Like I told the amateur pugilist, by the time somebody's

desperate enough to come to us, things are a lot more complicated and a lot more people are involved."

Max barked a sharp laugh. "Let me tell you how complicated things are." He shared everything that had happened to him that day — meeting Melinda Corkille, chasing Melinda Corkille, discovering Curtis the beaten US Postal Service guy, punching Mr. Gold, and hearing the troubling confession of the Hull family's involvement.

Sandra fell into her chair and whispered, "Shit."

"Not a very womanly way to say it," Drummond said, "but I agree with the sentiment."

"There's no way to back out of this, is there?" Max asked.

Drummond shook his head. "You know better. When you get a name like Hull involved, there's no easy way clear."

"What's Hull want with this anyway?" Sandra asked.

"I don't know," Max said. "I just thought I was done with them the last time."

Drummond snickered. "They do own the building. They probably own half the town. You should expect to come in contact with them once in a while."

"Shut up. I'm sick of hearing your little cracks all the time. It's been a tough enough day without having to hear a dead stand-up comic — and not even a good one at that."

"Easy now. I'm just trying to calm things, and maybe help you all get a little perspective."

"How do you think you're doing?" Max yelled, his face tight and red, his breathing heavy.

Drummond rose toward the ceiling with a placating grin. "Okay, now, there's no need to raise your voice. I'll just go see if I can find Corkille. I'll come back tomorrow morning when you've blown off some steam." And then he was gone.

Max looked at Sandra, the shock on her face matching his. "I can't believe he just backed down like that," Max said.

"Maybe he meant what he said. He was just trying to calm you down and since it isn't working, he left."

"Maybe." Max let out a long sigh. "Take the rest of the day off. I'll see you back home for dinner."

"You sure? There's plenty I can do."

"I just want to be alone."

Sandra leaned in to kiss Max but when he didn't turn to face her, she pecked his cheek and said, "I'll see you later. And don't forget, I love you."

"I love you, too," Max whispered as she walked out the door.

After a few minutes, he poured another shot of whiskey, held it to his lips, and inhaled its rich aroma. Then he tossed the fire liquid into the back of his throat, forced it down and let out a loud, "Ahhhh." Though he never grew fond of whiskey's sharp taste, after seeing Curtis, he welcomed the drink's numbing effect.

Max closed his eyes and fell asleep.

An hour later, he awoke, his heart pounding as he adjusted to his surroundings. He hated falling asleep by accident. He found the whole experience disorienting, at best.

"That's the problem with this case," he said to the empty office. And though he received no response other than silence, he knew he was right. The whole case, in the few hours they had worked on it, disoriented him. Not a single aspect of it seemed solid. Nothing but questions. Who are the Corkilles? What's with the painting that nobody knows about but everybody knows about? Why would Howard Corkille disappear? What did Melinda fear? And on and on.

And now the Hull family was involved.

Disorienting.

Max sat at his desk and tried to pick out a single detail he could count as fact. "Curtis wasn't the intended target," he said and wrote it on a piece of paper. A few seconds of thought, and he crossed out the sentence. Though it was probably true, he couldn't say it for a fact.

He crumpled the paper and tossed it across the room. *Tomorrow,* he thought. He closed up the office and headed home.

* * *

When Max entered the kitchen and saw their little table decked out with tablecloth, candlelight, wine, wineglasses, and two combo meals from Wendy's, all of the day's pressures erupted into laughter. He flopped into his chair, laughing himself silent, while Sandra looked on from the hall doorway. After a few deep breaths and a few lapses into more laughter, Max wiped his eyes, walked to his wife, and gave her a firm, loving kiss.

"You're wonderful," he said.

"I know. It's not my fault, though. I was just born this way." He kissed her again, and they sat down to dinner.

They ate in comfortable silence for a while. Then Max burped and said, "Tomorrow, I'm quitting the Corkille case."

"Okay."

Max hesitated. "You're not going to try to dissuade me? Tell me I have to stay on for the money or the business or whatever?"

"I think the name Hull changes this enough."

"I'd be lying if I said I didn't agree, but I've stood up to them before."

Sandra sipped her wine with a calm hand, but there was nothing relaxed in her posture. "I was with you through all that. I was a target of theirs, too. And even if I didn't see this man today all bruised and beaten up, I know the type of people we're talking about. Wealthy, powerful people who murder detectives and cast spells on their ghosts. People who have a long, nasty history in this town. So, if you don't want to risk getting any more contact with them, I completely understand."

"Well, good," Max said, confused at why he thought he should be arguing with her. "We do need the money, though."

"Then stay on the case. I'm going to support you either way. I'm just saying that I understand why you wouldn't want to deal with Hull again."

Max wanted to scream. His chest felt constricted; his mouth dry. "I hate this."

"Hull?"

"Everything. I just want to be left alone, do my research, and enjoy our life together. But ever since we moved down here, we keep having stuff like this happen."

"It wasn't any better in Michigan."

"I know. It's just — I don't know. I don't know how to say any of this." He knew what he wanted to say — that she should stop working for him — but he couldn't do it. After she had set up this silly dinner for him, after she had offered her support, after she had done what little work he asked of her, how could he let her go?

Taking his hand, Sandra led him into the living room. She sat him on the couch and nestled under his arm. She smelled wonderful — a natural smell as if the wind had brushed her with the trees' aroma, a smell as warm and secure as a thick blanket.

If he quit the case, the other ghost cases would disappear. He wasn't faring any better with the living. His fledgling business would die. The burning red number on his computer confirmed that.

Sandra stroked his arm and said, "You know the last time we went up against Hull things turned out okay."

"Yeah, and we figured out back then that we can't keep running."

"It's sure an easy habit to fall back into, though, right?"

"You knew before I walked in here, didn't you?"

"Knew what?"

Max kissed the top of her head. "You knew I'd want to quit the job, and you knew that eventually, if I talked about it even a little bit, I'd talk myself right back into doing it. We need the money, we need the work, and we can't run away. You know me that well."

"Maybe," she said with a toying chuckle.

"Then tell me this much. Since I'm staying on in this mess, how am I going to solve it? Every aspect of it is nothing but tangles of questions."

Sandra sat up, leaving her hand on his chest, and looked

upon him with incredulous eyes. "You've drunk too much tonight, if you can't figure that part out."

"What'd I say?"

"Honey, tomorrow, you go hit the library. You do what you know best. Research. It doesn't matter which thread of this case you follow. Pick one and start working."

Max nodded. She was right. He should've gone to the library from the first. Maybe it was the financial pressure or maybe the eagerness brought on by a new client, but he had jumped into the fray too fast. He needed to learn the background, research the names, know who these people actually were. Tomorrow, he would start this case over again.

"You're a smart gal," he said and planted a strong kiss on her lips.

"I know that, too," she said, returning the kiss.

Despite the long day, the stress, and the alcohol, Max felt his body stirring at Sandra's touch. They spent a few minutes on the couch kissing like teenagers until finally she pulled back and said, "I've missed you."

"Huh?"

"That's the first time you've really kissed me like that in I don't know how long. This business has got you so worked up, you just haven't been, well, you."

"I hadn't realized. Maybe I have been a bit distant. I sometimes feel crowded by Drummond and you in the office all the time. Not to say that —"

"Don't over-think it, hon. Especially right now," she said and started kissing him again. Max didn't need any more motivation. They went to the bedroom, grasping and gasping, feeling young and fresh, each excited by the other — it had been too long since they did more than just be physically satisfied. When they finished that night, they held each other until they fell asleep.

# Chapter 7

WAKE FOREST UNIVERSITY'S Z. Smith Reynolds Library — for Max, the place had become a refuge from the world. It's bright, open study areas balanced with the crowded stacks overstuffed with books. It was the greatest knowledge buffet, and Max loved it.

He launched right into his investigation, confidence and hope blending with his sense of purpose. He started with a computer search of the name Howard Corkille. After receiving over two hundred thousand hits, he narrowed it by adding "North Carolina." This returned twenty-seven thousand. He checked out a few links — some lawyer in California writing about a deal with NCU, a baker in Florida born in North Carolina, and a bar mitzvah blog. Adding "Winston-Salem" brought the number down to one hundred twenty-seven.

"That's better," he said, garnering a scowl from a young gal working at a desk surrounded by books and papers.

Following several links to start and using that information for deeper research, Max learned much about the Corkille family over the course of that morning. Edwin Corkille, born and raised in Ireland, fled the country after being accused of murdering a woman he had been promised to for marriage. He insisted on his innocence but could see that nobody wanted to believe him. So he ran.

His family was wealthy, and when he arrived in New York, he used some of his funds to purchase land in North Carolina. "Then things turn murky," Max said as he wrote down the information. Something had occurred within a decade because the next references to Edwin Corkille involved an involuntary dissolution of property. Several banks fought over what few assets he had left. In the end, he was broke.

The American Corkilles had no contact with their Irish family, and as a result, found no help to regain their standing. They became a working-class family, struggling to survive, finding life in the military during the Civil War (and finding death as well). Yet no mention of new fortunes could be found.

Max re-read what he had found detailing the last few decades. The Corkille name was little known except for acreage sales from the property Melinda now lived in and a few mentions of Melinda's involvement with the Second Harvest Food Bank — a charity providing food for the impoverished. Of course, if all the Corkille's money came from selling art forgeries, that type of success would not be found written about in old newspaper articles.

Yet something bothered Max. Something didn't feel right about the sudden re-emergence of Corkille wealth. Art forgery might be lucrative, but the kind of money the Corkille estate appeared to be worth could not have been made that fast. "At least, I don't think it can," he said provoking a hiss from the student looking no closer to finishing her paper.

Max wanted to find a specific reference to Howard Corkille but nothing online provided help. With pleasure, he culled a list of books on art forgery and began searching the stacks. While the computer made life easier, it had also taken away many small joys. The tactile experience of researching book after book in the quiet intensity of a library was just one, but it was one that touched Max every day.

Another joy of library research — discovering new parts of the immense building. Max found the books on art forgery (both history and, amazingly, how-to) in a lovely wood-paneled room with large reading chairs and a warm atmosphere. He settled down with his finds and delved in like a giddy child.

"You won't find him there," a distinct voice said.

Max didn't need to look up to know who stood before him — Mr. Modesto, the Hull family representative.

"May I sit?" Modesto asked.

With a huff, Max closed his book and gestured to the empty chair opposite him. Modesto looked much the same as the last time they had spoken — when Max wrested control of his office space from the Hull Family and threatened to expose them if anything should ever happen to him. A well-groomed, well-dressed man, Modesto's features had evolved for maximum intimidation. Max sat straight but inside he cringed.

"What do you want?" he asked.

Modesto pointed to the art forgery books. "John Myatt is considered by many the greatest art forger of the twentieth century. In the '90s, he was convicted for passing off his own creations as lost Renoirs, Picassos, and Modiglianis. He said he never did it for profit but out of some crazed, perfectionist's desire to create near-perfect art. After he served his time, he started painting again — his own work this time. You can buy it today for around fifty to a hundred thousand dollars a painting. Not bad for a former fraud."

Max tossed the book aside. "Gee, thanks. Now I don't have to read that one."

"Elmyr de Hoy was considered the number two art forger of the same time. He died in 1976, otherwise, who knows what may have happened? Orson Welles made a pretentious documentary on the man."

"It's called 'F for Fake,' I read all about it."

"There's a famous tale about Picasso. He is shown several paintings. He dismisses them. 'They are all fakes,' he says. His friend says, 'But Pablo, I saw you paint these.' Picasso smiles a devilish smile and says, 'I can fake a Picasso as well as anybody.'"

Crossing his arms, Max said, "Whatever you want, I don't want a part of it."

"And then there's Han van Meegeren — possibly the most famous art forger of all time. He was Dutch, born around 1889, and well-known for his Vermeers. He made a 'Christ at Emmaus' that sold for six million dollars. Then he sold a Vermeer fake to a German art collector by the name of Hermann Göring. Things didn't go too well for him after that."

"Do you have a point?" Max said, knowing he sounded impetuous and wishing his stomach wasn't flipping in fear.

Modesto leaned in and said, "All those famous forgers, and not one of them ever knew, ever spoke of, ever even heard of Howard Corkille. Do you know why? Because the truly great art forgers are like the truly great criminals. They are never known. They don't get caught. They don't go to jail. They don't get books written about them. They are ghosts."

This caught Max. He wanted to throw some wiseass comment at Modesto just to tick off the proper man, but he couldn't say a word. Embarrassed that he hadn't come to the conclusion himself and stunned that it would come from Modesto, Max piled his books, stood, and walked towards the exit. He moved fast in hopes of getting away before his legs gave out. He really didn't want to know what Modesto was leading up to.

"Wait, please," Modesto said, following Max into the hall. Max pushed the elevator's call button and considered the stairs, but the narrow stairwell on the right echoed the ascent of two talkative students. Modesto blocked Max's way. "I'll follow you all day, if you make me. And I do know where your office is and your home. So, why not listen to me?"

Impatience, anger, fear — it all swirled within Max. But Modesto was right. If the Hulls wanted him to tell Max something, it would be told. So, with a curt nod, Max walked back into the warm room and sat in the first chair he came upon.

"Thank you," Modesto said, but like everything that came out of his mouth, this sounded threatening. "First, Mr. Hull wishes you to know that he is not the one behind what you saw yesterday."

"You mean the man you had beaten up thinking it was me?"

"That was Mr. Gold's doing. In an eager attempt to display his loyalties, Mr. Gold over-enthusiastically interpreted his instructions. You do recall how Mr. Hull insists on his instructions being followed properly?"

"Of course."

"I will see that Mr. Gold understands quite clearly the error he has made. It won't happen again. Mr. Hull wants you to know that he fully abides by our previous agreements."

Now Max understood. Modesto was here to smooth over any bad feelings Max had over the Gold incident. Hull feared Max would be angry and release the old journal he had copies of, the journal of the Hull family that documented centuries of corruption, manipulation, and witchcraft. This was all about protecting themselves.

"Don't worry," Max said like a benevolent king. "I won't harm you over this. Just see that it doesn't happen again."

"You have my word," Modesto said through gritted teeth.

"Then I think we're done." Max stood.

"One more item."

Max thrust an exasperated glare at Modesto, but the man's stern face reminded Max just how dangerous he could be. "What is it?"

"I must deliver this," Modesto said, handing over an ivory-colored envelope. "I've been instructed to tell you that the letter is not to be opened until you are in the presence of your wife and Mr. Drummond." Coming from anyone else, Max would have been shocked by this statement. But since it was a Hull who had cursed Drummond, who had bound his ghost to Max's office, and who had fought to stop Max from releasing him, Modesto's words were natural.

Max grabbed the envelope and pocketed it without ever taking his eyes off of Modesto. Perhaps it was the mentioning of Sandra and Drummond. Perhaps it was Modesto's incessant air of superiority — even when attempting to apologize for nearly killing a man. Perhaps it was simply the fear of dealing in any way with the Hull family once more. Whatever the case, Max's head spun in fury while his stomach threatened to revolt. His emotions churned with conflict as much as his body, and through taut lips, he said, "I don't ever want to see you again."

Modesto rose to his full height and looked down upon Max. "I appreciate your displeasure in having to meet. Rest assured the sentiment is mutual. However, as I am the top representative for Mr. Hull, I can assure you, we will be in contact again. No matter what you threaten, Mr. Hull will not entrust these delicate matters to another person. As you've seen with Mr. Gold, most others cannot be counted upon to execute instructions properly. I hope you understand the nature of this refusal and will not use it against Mr. Hull."

Modesto bent slightly and walked away. Fuming and helpless, Max watched him go. He pulled out the envelope, flipped it over, and set his finger at the edge to tear it open.

But he stopped.

Printed on the back were the words: NOT TO BE OPENED UNTIL IN THE PRESENCE OF MRS. PORTER AND MR. DRUMMOND. As much as Max wanted to raise a middle finger to Hull's instructions, he knew that doing so would be a bad move at this point. The time to fight back was when he held the most advantage. Besides, whatever this was all about, it was important enough to risk public exposure.

He put the envelope away, gathered his things, and headed back to the office. When he arrived, Sandra took one look, sat him down, and said, "Guess it didn't go well."

Max explained about Modesto's visit and placed the envelope on the table. Drummond shrugged. "At least the bastards haven't forgotten me. I ought to go haunt them for a few years. Just clank around their mansion, make sure nobody gets a decent night's sleep."

"I'll buy you a new set of chains," Max said.

Drummond chuckled. "I think the old, rusty ones have a better tone, but thanks for the offer."

"So," Sandra said, "are you going to open it?"

Max slid the envelope toward her. "You do it." She pulled back from the desk, her eyes narrowing on the envelope as if it might rear back and attempt to bite her.

"They want you to open it, though."

"Yes, but the instructions don't say anything specifically about who opens it. So, screw them. They forgot to be that clear, I say the heck with it."

"Okay," she said, snatched the envelope and tore it open. She read in silence, her face giving away nothing as to its contents.

"Hey, Sweets," Drummond said, "you going to share?"

With a devilish grin, she said, "The instructions were to open it in our presence. Doesn't say anything about reading it out loud."

"Oh, if only I were alive."

Max snatched the letter from Sandra. "Ease it back, you two." With a firm snap of the paper, he read:

> *It is with great pleasure that I cordially invite Mr. and Mrs. Maxwell Porter and Mr. Marshall Drummond to supper with me this Wednesday at seven o'clock.*
>
> *Please dress as befits the occasion. Should the day and time be unavailable, please contact Mr. Modesto at your earliest convenience so other arrangements can be determined.*
>
> *I look forward to our first meeting.*
>
> *— Terrance Hull*

Drummond hovered behind Max's shoulder. When he finished reading, he spoke for everyone when he said, "Well, that's not good at all."

# Chapter 8

WEDNESDAY MORNING BEGAN with strong coffee and a headache. Max did his best to ignore the dread building within like a hardening concrete block making every step a struggle, but with the Hull dinner only ten hours away, he found it impossible to think about much else. He tried searching the internet for more on Corkille but he couldn't concentrate.

Across his desk, he watched Sandra immersed in Corkille estate papers, criminal record searches, and other routine research. A fleeting sensation of peace passed through him. She glanced up, perhaps sensing his attention, and threw one of her casual but devastating smiles.

Drummond burst in and, with a clap of his hands, said, "So, we got the big dinner tonight. Too bad I can't actually eat anything anymore. Rich people know how to throw a spread. This'll probably be the best meal you've ever eaten, and I'm going to have to watch. You know, I'll bet that's why the bastard wants me there — torture me with things like that."

Grabbing his coat and coffee, Max said, "I'm going to see Melinda Corkille."

"Something I said?"

"I'm not spending the day fretting over Hull."

"Who's fretting? I think it's going to be a great ol' time. Eat the guy's food, insult him a few ways, hear whatever stupid threats he feels like making, and shine him on. Trust me, there's nothing more satisfying than undercutting some snobby ass like his. He's got a whole plan in his head of what he'll say and how we'll react. They hate it when we screw that kind of thing up. It'll be fun."

To Sandra, Max said, "Melinda Corkille's the only direct connection to any of this we still have. I've got to talk with her.

Besides," he added toward Drummond, "whatever Hull's going to say, you know it's going to be about this painting. If I can get any information from Melinda, it'll help us tonight."

"Good idea," Drummond said. "And don't worry. I'll find Howard eventually. We'll have more leads soon."

"Let me just finish up, and I'll join you," Sandra said.

"No," Max said. "I think it's best if I go alone. This lady is touchy. I think we'll scare her away if we come with a whole gang."

"Two is not a gang."

"You know what I mean. If this goes well, I'll bring you both next time."

Sandra kissed Max, concern scrunching her features. "Be careful. And don't go chasing cars again."

"I'll be good," he said, but he didn't smile.

The drive down seemed longer than before. Max's mind zipped back and forth between Hull's impending dinner and Sandra's strangling presence. Apprehensive about the former and guilty about the latter, Max saw little room to maneuver. The dinner would come and go, and he knew he'd have to handle whatever happened. But Sandra — that was a problem that time would not fix on its own.

In fact, if he just let it be, it would only compound and possibly form the root that could destroy them. That's how divorces happened. Little things couples tried to ignore, tried to bury through hot nights, festered until they became monumental, until they led to actions neither spouse ever thought the other capable of.

"Like visiting Melinda Corkille by yourself because she's got your blood going? Little things like that, Max?"

The steering wheel had no answer — and neither did Max. He stared at the straight, unchanging road and promised himself that this would be the last time. Not that he had done anything wrong — but he'd had plenty of guilty thoughts. He just didn't want those thoughts to lead to actions. At the next opportunity, he promised himself, he would hash things out with Sandra, fix things, get them back on the right track. And not just a little talk like the previous night. They needed to find the root of this problem and kill it so it never grew back.

Ten minutes later, he pulled into the drive and parked his car, noticing a new rattle from the engine that assured him of a hefty mechanic's bill in the coming weeks. Melinda must have heard the rattle as well because she opened the front door and walked out as Max stepped from the car. She wore old jeans and a low-cut top that left little to be discovered. He fought to keep his eyes on her face.

"You again," she said with a playful half-grin.

"I'm sorry to bother you, but I just need a few minutes of your time."

"There's nothing I can tell you."

"Please. You don't have to give me loads of information or betray any family secrets. I just need a little help from you to point me in the right direction."

"You said you were writing a book on art forgers?"

"That's right."

She snapped her fingers and pointed at him. "See, that's a lie. Why should I help you out when you've begun this whole thing with a lie?"

Opening his arms like a thief claiming innocence, he said, "I admit it. I lied. But you have to admit, too, that you'd never have spoken to me, if I had told you the truth."

"Depends on what the truth is."

"Well, the truth is that I've been hired to find that painting for you."

"For me?"

"I was told to find the painting, find you, and put the two together."

"And who hired you?"

"I can't tell you that."

"That's really too bad. You almost had my interest." She turned away.

"Wait, please. I don't know what's so special about this

painting, but you're clearly in it deep, and you'll get buried, if you're not careful."

"Lucky for me, I'm a careful person."

"Melinda, please —"

She placed her hand on the door and said, "Good-bye, Mr. Porter. Do not come here again."

Desperation took hold. Max blurted out, "You don't want to be messing with the Hulls. They're dangerous."

Melinda froze. Her seductive yet light lips became a hard, cold line. "What do you know about them?"

"Let me in. I'll tell you all about it."

Any sense of wild youth vanished from Melinda. She looked meek and even vulnerable. She stepped back into the house, leaving the front door open.

Max walked into the foyer and tried not to betray his awe. He did not often step into such a wealthy home. Dark wood floors led up a small step into the main foyer which was garnered with a baby-grand piano. The walls were old Southern white, a summer breeze color that whispered of a South that had died long ago.

"This way," she said, passing through a wide arch into a lush living room — thick sofas, a brick fireplace, and paintings on every wall — Max lacked the skill to know if they were authentic or not. Everything he saw looked valuable and vibrant. Even the plants.

Max stood next to a deep red sofa, unsure if he should sully it with his common pants. Even as he had these thoughts, another part of him complained in his head — *Since when do you care about rich assholes? Sit down and take command of things.*

Since when? Easy answer — since he saw that red number on his computer screen.

"Please, sit," she said. Max settled on the sofa's edge and noticed a large plant in front of a narrow door — the rich hiding the broom closet. Concern over his pants itched stronger than before. Melinda slid onto the opposite sofa, her legs tucked under in a pose reminiscent of a college girl, and continued, "So, Mr. Porter, enlighten me about the Hulls."

"I worked for Hull a year ago. He was a dangerous man, part of a dangerous family that shrouds itself in secrecy."

"My family likes secrets, too," she said with a wink.

"This is serious. These people can cause a lot of pain."

Melinda chuckled — a soft, bitter sound that she managed to infuse with a salacious undertone. "You're sweet to be so concerned, but you've only lived here for what? A little over a year? My family has been in North Carolina for generations. I think we understand things down here a bit better."

"But —"

"Do you know why I have this house? I mean, do you understand that every inch of this place was paid for by art forgeries? And yet, I still own it."

"I've been told the best art forgers never get caught. I couldn't find a single word about Howard Corkille."

"That's part of it. An important part. The other is attached to being the best. In order to succeed, you must be able to pass off your work for profit."

"And Howard was good at that as well?"

"A genius. But, you see, the two go together — getting collectors and museums to buy your forgeries and keeping all knowledge of you and your involvement a secret. Even now, all these years later, should it come out that many of the prized works hanging in museums throughout the world were Corkille fakes, I'd lose every dime I ever had. I hope this makes it clear why I don't wish to have an in-depth study done on my family's history."

"This painting," Max said, not knowing what to say but wanting to keep her talking, "the 'Morning in Red,' why are you messing with Hull over it?"

"I'm not."

"You practically jumped when I mentioned his name and now you suddenly don't care about him?"

"I didn't say that. I'm just not involved with Hull over that painting." Despite the young girl clothes and poses, her weary voice and judicious gaze aged her before Max's eyes. "We have other issues at work."

"Well, if I'm not being rude, I'd advise you to have no dealings with Hull at any time, of any kind. That family is destructive, at best, and powerfully so. Whatever you think you're doing with them will hurt you in the long run. I learned this the hard way. Please, trust me on this. You'd best stay away from them."

"How cute. You truly want to be chivalrous."

Max knew he should leave. Though Melinda passed with ease between being a naïve doe and a prowling hunter, Max saw danger in either state. She played both with perfect pitch. The subtle and direct looks she threw at him from behind her hair, casually placed in its most seductive position, flooded him with testosterone and made thinking clearly an impossible task. The only thought he could manage — *leave, leave, leave.*

As if the idea had formed that instant, Melinda sauntered toward Max and bent down with the obvious intent of letting him view her breasts. "We have a few choices," she said, moving closer, her lips near his. Hints of perfume mixing with body heat pressed in the air. "We can continue to tell each other partial truths and partial lies, we can go about our separate interests and know that we'll cross paths sometime soon, or we can stop all the games, go upstairs, and you can do whatever you desire." With the tip of her tongue, she touched his lips. Then she pulled back and turned away. "I know which I choose," she said and removed her shirt in one swift motion. Her smooth back lacked a single blemish. Over her bare shoulder, she added, "I'll wait upstairs."

When she left the room, making sure to drop the shirt on the floor, Max did not move. His brain had shut down and struggled to reboot. His heart pounded in a fear only matched by the longing in his groin. He felt guilty for being hard and stupid for even imagining following this crazy girl. Drummond would tell him to sleep with her but never forget that she's only trying to distract him from the case. Maybe.

Or maybe, despite all his big talk, Drummond would race to the car — he cares about Sandra a little bit. Max, however, cared about Sandra infinitely. No amount of marital bickering would change that.

With his body cooling down, his heart slowing, his brain function returning, Max willed himself to stand and walked out of that house. His eyes lingered on Melinda's discarded shirt and he imagined her upstairs, draped across her bed, waiting for him. Never had a woman come on to him like that. He could feel a pulling in his body as if the mere scent of Melinda that dwindled in the air could call him up like a siren's song. He had been wrong to leave Sandra behind. He needed her as a shield against this seductive woman.

He stopped by the baby-grand piano and pictured his lovely wife. *That's who matters. The other thoughts are just hormones.* He stepped outside, got to his car, and let out a long breath. Pushing his foot hard on the gas, he promised he would not make that mistake again.

# Chapter 9

"I KNOW YOU'RE NERVOUS," Sandra said as they drove to the Hull family estate, "but try to relax. You won't be thinking clearly if you're all stressed out."

"What's that supposed to mean? That I 'won't be thinking clearly'. I can make clear decisions."

Drummond, floating in the backseat, said, "Hey, relax. You know that's not what she meant."

"I didn't ask you."

Tense silence filled the car. They drove out of Winston-Salem, south on Route 77 toward Lake Norman. Max tried to focus on the dinner, on the case, on anything but Sandra, Drummond, or Melinda.

He peeked at Drummond in the rear-view mirror just in time to see Drummond's head stretch backward and to hear him scream. Sandra jumped at the sound, took one glance back, and yelled, "Pull over! Pull over!"

As Max edged to the shoulder and slowed down, he swore he could see through Drummond as if the ghost had become less substantial than usual. Drummond held his elongated head with one hand and strained his muscles but still growled out his pain. With his free hand, he pointed behind them.

"What is this? What's going on?" Max asked.

"I don't know," Sandra said. "I've never seen a ghost do anything like this before."

With a great effort, Drummond pointed and said, "Back!"

Max hit the hazard lights, set the car in reverse, and eased back along the shoulder. In just a few feet, Drummond's head returned to its normal shape, and he seemed to be in less pain. A few more feet and the ghost had become solid in appearance once again.

Max stopped the car and turned around in his seat. "What the heck just happened? You okay?"

Drummond rubbed the back of his head. "Damn, I wish I could drink. My mouth is begging for a whiskey right now."

"He's alright," Sandra said with a relieved chuckle.

"Look at that. You do care."

"Don't push it."

"Cute, you two," Max said, "but nobody's answered my question. What just happened?"

Repositioning his hat, Drummond said, "It looks like I can't go any further. I've heard talk about this but figured it was just ghost superstitions — hoped it was, at least."

"What *what* was?"

"A ghost exists in two realms. There's the ghostly realm where I found Corkille. It's like a separate plane or world. That world, the ghost world, it's enormous and I can go anywhere in it I need to go.

"Here, however, in the corporeal world, it's different. The rumor is that every ghost is sort of tethered to the place they died. I guess it's true. I can't go too far from the office without a heck of a lot of pain."

"You're okay now, though, right?"

"I think so."

Sandra said, "There's a third world, too, don't forget. You can always *move on* to there."

Drummond looked away like a boy avoiding punishment. "I'm not ready for that."

"Now what you talking about?" Max asked.

"Heaven and Hell," Sandra said. "If you believe in them, that is. Call it the real afterlife. Being a ghost means you're not letting go, but once you do, you move on to that third world realm. You find out what really happens."

"Can we just turn around?" Drummond said, crossing his arms.

Checking his watch, Max clicked his tongue. "That's going to be a problem. We can't go all the way back to the office and then back to Lake Norman and still be on time. For that matter, Hull wanted you there, too, and you know that guy is nutty about his exact orders being followed."

"It'll be fine," Sandra said. "He won't even know Drummond's not there. He can't see ghosts, can he?"

"I don't know."

"No," Drummond said. "I don't think he can. But he knows about ghosts and witches and all of it. And that means he knew I couldn't actually be there tonight. This part of the evening was merely to show me he's still out of my reach. The bastard is just rubbing my death into my face."

"You might be right."

"Don't worry about me. I'll go to the ghost realm and use that to get back to the office. The two worlds don't synch exactly, so I'm sure I'll be back long before you."

"But —" Sandra started to speak, but before she could utter her objection, Drummond had disappeared.

"I guess that's that," Max said, pulling the car back to the highway.

When they arrived Max first noticed that, for a mansion, the place was small. Elegant, yes, but not the sprawling acreage one would expect from a family rich enough to own half the state. As they walked toward the front door, a young, blonde man wearing a flawless black suit stepped out to greet them.

"Mr. and Mrs. Porter," he said, his drawl smooth and refined, "it is a pleasure to meet you. I'm Terrance Hull."

Max had to grip Sandra's hand to avoid tripping. This was Hull? This kid whose face barely grew a whisker was the one he had feared so much?

Hull led them into the house with a mock laugh. "You're not the first to be surprised at my youth," he said. "Or my informalities. I apologize if you expected a butler. I do have help at my main home, but this place is usually used as a miniature vacation spot, and as such, I don't often want staff bothering me."

"It's a lovely home," Sandra said, though Max thought she growled more than spoke.

Hull didn't appear to notice. "Thank you," he said, taking

their coats. The inside of the home was immaculate. Every piece of crystal, every gold trim, every framed picture, shined in its cleanliness. Light played against these objects, brightening the house and warming it. If Hull didn't employ the help, he must have at least sent Mr. Modesto ahead to clean up the place. Max couldn't picture Hull working the elbow grease to keep up this level of clean.

As Hull walked down the hall, Max glanced back. The front door had been left open. He went to shut it when he noticed there were no locks on the door. None. Once before he had seen such a thing — the office of a woman who turned out to be a real, spell-casting witch. Drummond told him the witch never needed locks because nobody dared to rob her. Not only did Hull not have locks, he didn't even bother closing the door. Max felt that old fear creeping back into his stomach.

The dining room's beauty surpassed any room Max had ever stepped foot in — hardwood floors reflecting like mirrors, candlelight twinkling like stars, and a simple but elegant meal served on shining silver. With swift grace, Hull pulled out a chair for Sandra, indicated a chair for Max, and then took his own seat at the head of the table. The food — duck with mushrooms in a white wine sauce — filled the room with its gentle aroma.

"It's not often I get the chance to cook for anybody," Hull said, his pleasure warming the room like the candlelight. "Please, enjoy the food."

Max's anger strengthened with every pleasantry. This was the man who had tried to hurt Max and Sandra on several occasions. Did he really think so little of them that he expected Max to bow down before the almighty wealthy despite the past? Sandra rested her hand on Max's knee, patting him to stay silent, *stay calm*. If not for that soft hand, he would've jumped to his feet and let his mouth loose. Instead, he ate the sumptuous meal and tried not to enjoy it.

He lost on that last account. The food was damn good.

"Is Mr. Drummond here?" Hull asked after a few minutes.

"No," Max said. "But you already knew that."

"I was not certain whether the spatial limitations were true or just a myth. Next time I'll be sure to utilize a location closer to Spruce Street."

"Next time?" Sandra perked up.

"I think so," Hull said and rose to his feet. He paced around the dining room as he spoke, his agitation palpable. "I suppose there's no point in being coy. After all, it's not often that I call somebody for dinner, is it?"

"We wouldn't know," Max said, but something ticked in his mind. He suspected Hull *never* had guests for dinner — certainly never in this way. Alone and without even the minimum servants. Not even Mr. Modesto.

"I prefer anonymity. However, in this case, I don't think you would be convinced by a letter. In fact, a letter from me might make the whole idea ludicrous."

"What idea is that?"

"That you come work for me again." Sandra blurted out a shocked laugh while Max stared at the man, too stunned for more. Hull continued, "Before you say a word, let me speak. I fully recall how things stand between us and have full respect for the threat you hold over me. That is another reason why I've been forced to present myself to you this way. As to why I wish to hire you — you're a smart man. You know what this is about."

Max put his fork onto the plate with a hard clank. "The painting. *Morning in Red.* Right?"

"Exactly. Since you're already searching for it, I simply wish to have you locate it for me. Of course, I'll be happy to pay you double your normal fee. And I can assure you, this will in no way impact or alter our previous situation."

Max shook his head, unable to talk for fear of shouting. Sandra, however, did not hold back. She bolted to her feet, pointing at Hull like a stern mother reprimanding an insolent child. "How dare you even think of such a moronic idea. How dare you. You think your money can buy us off? You think we're greedy? Of course you do. Look at this place. You only understand money. Well, your wealth won't help you here. Our answer is no. Emphatically, *No*."

"There's no need to get upset."

"You think you can threaten people's lives and not have them be upset? You're a monster."

"Did I really *ruin* your life? Would you prefer to go back to Michigan, have your husband go on trial for embezzlement, spend another year freezing with little heat in the house and no husband in your bed? It seems that through my former employment, you've made a big step upward in your life."

Max held Sandra's shoulders to keep her from raising a fist at Hull — and possibly using it. Seething, she struggled against him, but he held her still. To Hull, he said, "Thank you for dinner. As to your offer, I think you can figure out our answer."

Hull raised a glass of wine, sipped, and in a quiet, threatening voice, said, "That's a shame because I will have that painting, and if you are not helping me, then you are harming me. Do not get in my way. No matter what guarantees you think you hold against me, there are some things that are worth the risk. I promise you, this is one. Whoever got you into this, I urge you to sever those ties. Leave this whole affair."

Sandra made one last lunge, but Max held her firm. Hull oozed condescension, and for a fleeting moment, Max considered letting his wife take a swipe at the man. He held back, though — partly because it was the right move to make, but partly because something still gnawed at him about the entire evening and the way Hull had behaved, something seemed out-of-place when compared to the Hull he had come to know through Mr. Modesto.

The drive home consisted of Sandra venting her anger for most of the trip until Max began laughing. "What?" she asked. "Why are you laughing?"

"You were the one telling me to stay calm all night."

Sandra began a protest and then filled the car with her own laughter. And though the weight of the evening pressed heavier on Max than at any time throughout that day, he found the release of Sandra's tensions a release for himself as well. He drove the rest of the way with a smile.

The next morning Max and Sandra entered the office holding hands and giggling over nothing in particular. Drummond sat behind the big desk — his face drawn, his arms crossed.

"You couldn't stop by here last night? Let me know what happened? I worked hard for you and you made me wait until this morning? And to top it off, you're all cutesy together."

With a light-hearted grin, Sandra said, "We're sorry. It was a long, late night, and we just needed —"

"I know what you needed. That doesn't change the fact —"

Max motioned Drummond out of his chair. "You're acting like my mother. We couldn't make it back, so just accept it at that. We're sorry if it inconvenienced you. Now, if you want, we'll be glad to tell you about all that happened."

"I'm listening."

Max delved into a recap of the evening. When he finished, Drummond's frown continued but now it was directed at the story and not the storyteller. "When you say Hull was a young man, was he really young or did he just look that way?"

"As far as I could tell, he was young."

"That's right. No more than thirty," Sandra added.

Drummond shook his head. "Then that wasn't Terrance Hull you were dining with. Hull was born sometime in the forties, maybe the fifties at the latest. He's got to be near sixty-years-old by now."

"Maybe this was Terrance Junior."

"Possibly, but I don't recall another Hull being born in the last few decades. If it happened, they've kept it a tight secret. Which isn't to say it didn't happen. These are the Hulls after all. I just find it disturbing that he picks a place for dinner he knows I can't go to when I'm one of the few people who knows what a Hull looks like."

Max said, "It doesn't matter. We turned him down and

we're not interested in his games. We'll find this painting before him and then we'll have the leverage."

Drummond clapped his hands. "Well, then, you're going to need what I have for you. I spent all night working my skills, and I have for you this present."

Drummond reached into the bookshelf wall and pulled something back. He shoved it into the client chair, his face glowing with pride. Max looked to Sandra whose expression told him little. "Well?" he finally said in frustration. "What's in the chair?"

Sandra said, "Howard Corkille."

"No," Drummond said. "That's the big news. This ghost, the one who hired us, he is not Howard Corkille."

# Chapter 10

MAX WATCHED THE EMPTY CHAIR as if he expected the ghost to spring before him. At that moment, he decided he hated art forgers and everything connected to them. "So, who is he?" he finally asked.

Drummond gestured to the chair. "This is Jasper Sullivan."

"And why are you pretending to be an old art forger?" Sandra asked before Max could clear his mind enough to do so. He bit back on a sharp remark.

As Sandra frowned at the response, Max snapped his fingers. "Well? What the heck is he saying?"

"Sorry," she said. "He says, 'Please, don't be mad. Please. I'm very sorry. It wasn't my intent to deceive you.'"

Max huffed. "You lied about who you are. That seems pretty intent on deception."

"'I know, I know. It's not like that, though. You see, I couldn't tell you the truth, but I'm prepared to tell you everything now.'"

"Because we've caught you."

"'Just listen, please.'"

Max looked to Drummond who signaled agreement. "Okay," Max said. "Let's hear it."

"'Much of what I told you was true,'" Sandra went on translating. "'I did live during the Great Depression. My wife, Clara, and I, we did suffer hard. I lost my job; I couldn't get work. All of that is true. I wasn't an art forger, obviously — just a clerk. Filing papers, keeping records, all sorts of paperwork, that kind of thing.

"'And ... I did buy a gun, and I did plan to kill myself. In fact, if you look up my name, you'll find my records indicate that I did commit suicide. Only I didn't.

"'Back then, you see, back during the Depression, sometimes people were removed from their homes rather quickly. Sometimes there were robberies, and sometimes there were deaths. The point is that sometimes people who shouldn't have certain items, who couldn't dream of affording such things, found them falling into their possession.'"

Impatient, Max gestured to the empty chair. "Is there a reason you find it so difficult to admit you had some stolen property? You're dead. The police can't get you now."

"'I still have my name, my pride. But I see you don't care about those things. Fine. Through connections that don't matter to this case, I came to own a certain painting.'"

"Just a wild guess, but was it called *Morning in Red?*"

"'No, but I'll get to that painting in a moment. The painting I had come across, well, I didn't know anything about art back then, but I was sure it was worth something. It wasn't by any artist I knew, it wasn't going to make me rich, but it was a beautiful painting and I thought to myself, *there must be some way to make some money from this.* That was a common thought back then — thought it about pretty much everything.

"'I put out word about the painting in the few places I knew. Then along came Howard Corkille.'"

Max didn't need Sullivan's nervous presentation to see where things went to next. After all, Corkille, the real Corkille, was an art forger. He, no doubt, recognized some worth in the painting and offered Jasper Sullivan a unique proposal. Corkille would make an identical painting, and they would sell it. Using Corkille's established connections, they would receive far more than Sullivan could acquire on his own, and splitting the profits even at an unfavorable 70/30 split would net Sullivan handsomely. Plus, Sullivan would retain the original painting.

Thinking about the other interested parties in this case, Max said, "I'm guessing Corkille sold the painting to a member of the Hull family."

"'William Hull.'"

Drummond patted the empty space as if consoling. "He was a dangerous man. You're not the first to be hurt by him nor the last ... that's right, William Hull was responsible for turning me into a ghost, too."

"Wait," Max said. "Hull killed you?"

"You knew that."

"Not you. Sullivan."

Sandra continued to translate. "'Not Hull directly. He had a hired hand take care of it. You see, he found out about the painting. I never learned how Hull knew. Maybe he knew his art that well, maybe Corkille screwed up doing the forgery, or maybe — probably — Corkille betrayed me. After all, I never saw the painting again. Corkille disappeared, the painting disappeared, and only Hull remained. It doesn't matter now, though. Hull figured it out. I'm sure you can imagine how he reacted.

"'I was frightened, and I wanted to protect Clara and my unborn child and, looking back, I was a bit of a coward. No, I was a lot of a coward. So, I did go to that tobacco field. I got drunk on cheap wine. And I did bring my gun. I planned to kill myself. I figured that would end Hull's interest in me and leave my family out of the matter.

"'But I couldn't do it. I couldn't pull the trigger. I sat in that field feeling the cold metal touching the skin on my head, and I kept picturing my dear Clara — how sad she would be when she found out what I had done. I saw how she would someday have to explain to my son what I had done. All I saw was pain. And I was afraid. I didn't know if there was an afterlife, but I figured if there was, I wouldn't be going anyplace good. And then I felt a hand cover mine. This hand that took hold of the gun, the one I told you saved me — the truth is that the hand belonged to Hull's man. He helped me pull the trigger.'"

Max jotted a few points down. "So, you and Howard Corkille try to pass off a forgery on Hull and it gets you killed. This certainly fills in some gaps, but you said the painting wasn't *Morning in Red.* So why did you hire us to find that one? And why are you coming clean now?"

"'I'm telling you all this because I did some checking of my own in the Other.'"

Drummond said, "He means the ghost world."

"I know what he means," Max said.

"'I came to you because you're the only ghost detective around. Or researcher, if you prefer. But as things started moving, I thought I ought to know more about you folks. So, I asked around about Drummond. When I learned of his being cursed by Hull and all, then I knew I could trust you with the truth.

"'As to the *Morning in Red* painting — I first heard of it about twenty years ago. Corkille caused my murder, and that's not something I can forgive. My wife spiraled into a sadness that claimed her. Once our son had reached fifteen, my Clara killed herself. My son, a boy I never met in life, became a violent and abusive man. Without his father to guide him, he turned to a criminal's life. So, you see, Corkille's damage to me went far beyond the theft of a painting. He destroyed my family. I spent many years looking for him in the Other. I wanted to hurt him, but he's always eluded me. And then a few decades ago, I heard he searched for this particular, odd painting.

"'That's how I learned about it — I heard Corkille wanted it. He's been looking hard — hard enough that I found out about it. So, whatever it is, it's important to him. Enough to get too noisy about it. It must be worth quite a lot and so I want it.'"

"You sent us to Melinda Corkille to get us started on the right track."

"'Yes.'"

Max walked the room with no destination. He just needed to move. He tapped his chin and licked his lips. "I'm confused. What do you want to do with this painting? You can't sell it. Even if I did it for you, it might not be worth all that much. Besides, money is worthless to you."

"'It's enough to deny Corkille what he is desperate to get. I don't know why he wants it, but I want him to have to come to me to get it. It may seem petty, I know, but if your life had turned out like mine, you'd spend hundreds of years plotting such revenge.'"

Drummond said, "Give the guy a break. As revenges go, this one is mild. I've seen enough blood-spattered walls to know that hatred can get real nasty."

Something was wrong. Why was Drummond acting so nice? Max focused on Drummond but couldn't get a sign from him. "Fine," he said. "You have anything else for us?"

""I don't think so. If I think of anything, I'll let you know. And I'll be available. Don't worry."

"We trust you," Drummond said. "You relax. We'll find that painting for you."

Sandra looked up from the chair. "He's gone."

"What's with you?" Max asked Drummond. "You're not really going for all that."

Drummond slid into the client chair, propped his feet on the desk, and opened his arms like a conqueror. "Of course not. But you've got to learn how to be nice sometimes. This guy, if we came in bullying him, he would've seen us like another one of Hull's men. He said it himself — he's a coward. I just played nice while you were being all aggressive."

"Are you saying we just played Good Cop/Bad Cop?"

"You didn't know that's what we were doing?"

Max turned away but he caught the amusement on Sandra's face. He tried not to get angry or have any reaction to his embarrassment. Drummond saved him by clapping his hands together once and jumping into the air. "Okay. I think we need to pay a few visits."

Sandra helped by following along with this get-back-to-work attitude. "What do you have in mind?"

Though Max did not look at Drummond, he heard the hesitation, and it chilled his skin. "Old Jasper there had a few good nuggets to share," Drummond said. "The one that I keep hearing is that all of this is tied to Hull. In particular, to William Hull. Did you notice the way Jasper reacted when we were talking about how Hull had me cursed?"

"What reaction?" Max said turning to Sandra.

She said, "I couldn't tell you with him sitting right here, but he got very tense. If he wasn't already a pale ghost, I'd have said he turned white."

Drummond slid behind Sandra and put both hands on her shoulders — not enough to cause pain but enough to make the contact known. "I think Hull might've done more to Jasper Sullivan than just kill him. He did it to me. Thanks again, by-the-way, to both of you for freeing me from that."

"You can thank me by letting go of my wife," Max said.

Drummond raised his hand up. "Sorry. Just friends."

"Get to the final point or I'll have you re-cursed." Every second in this case filled him with unease as if he walked on fragile crates knowing any wrong step could smash them open, and he had no idea if they contained soft pillows or jagged knives.

"My point is simply that if William Hull cursed Jasper, he would have used a witch — a particular witch whose daughter is continuing in the family tradition."

"No," Max said, picturing jagged knives.

"She's the one with the answers."

"She tried to kill me."

"She failed."

"I am not going to see her and act all nice so I can get some information from her. I won't do it."

Sandra grabbed the car keys. "I'll do it for you. Drummond'll come with me."

Drummond perked up. "Spend the day with a pretty gal like you? No problem. Don't worry, Max. I'll be a gentleman."

The two headed for the office door. Defeated, Max said, "Just hold on. Let me get my coat."

# Chapter 11

THE DOOR HAD A LOCK NOW. That was the first difference they noticed standing at the office of Dr. Connor, optometrist and witch. The second was the quiet.

Not absolute silence but a muted quiet strange for this area. Westgate Center Drive, with its numerous doctor's offices and outpatient facilities, ran somewhat parallel to Stratford Road — one of the busiest roads since it connected to Hanes Mall. Tons of restaurants and loads of shops, yet despite the steady number of passing cars and the occasional delivery truck, things remained quiet. Even the birds stopped chirping around Connor's office.

Though he had survived their last meeting, Max could not avoid the horrible, gut-churning sensation thoughts of Dr. Connor brought upon him. She was not somebody to mess around with. Whatever information she might have for them, he knew it would come with a price.

"Are you going in or not?" Drummond asked.

Sandra took hold of Max's hand. "It'll be okay."

"You don't know that," Max said, but he opened the door anyway. The darkness inside matched his fear — heavy and pressing. When they stepped inside, however, the mood lightened considerably. He had seen poverty before — desolation, dereliction, destruction, even blood and death. Until this moment, he never felt a sense of relief (and even a tinge of joy) at seeing such things.

The witch's office lay in ruin. Not because some tornado of ruthless vandals had swept through but rather out of neglect. Dust covered the few bits of furniture that remained. The shades were drawn, letting the sun peek in at odd angles. Empty food containers littered the floor as did the blood-markings of a half-completed spell (at least, Max thought it looked half-completed). A picture lay smashed in the corner next to a hole in the wall at about the height of an aggravated kick. An empty bottle of Jack Daniel's leaned against a half-empty bottle.

"Dr. Connor?" Sandra called.

Somebody stirred in the back. Sandra called out again, and this time they heard coughing before a bent lady shuffled toward them. A year ago, Dr. Connor had been a vibrant, frightening woman — young, powerful, and eager to use both to her advantage. Max looked upon her now with pity — she appeared to have aged twenty years or more in just one year.

When she saw her visitors, her face flushed with fierce venom. "You! Demon! You dare come back here. Just because you hurt me once, you think you can finish me off? I'll whip you to the ground," she said, raising her hands as if to hurl herself upon Max. She froze in that awkward position, her eyes searching, her ears perked. Then she let out a sinister smile. "You brought the ghost with you. Good. I'll smite all three of you. Send you to Hell where you belong."

All of the past few days burned through any sense of calm or fear Max had possessed. Before he could think about it, he let loose the fire. "You piece of trash," he said, showing no restraint. "You're the one that deserves Hellfire. You threaten my wife and my friend? You threaten me?"

"You destroyed my office. You broke my spell."

"That would be the spell you tried to kill me with."

"When others saw what you had done, I became a failed witch — tainted. I lost respect. I lost most of my business because of you. Who wants to get magic done by a tainted witch?"

"I doubt that's the whole problem. Look at yourself. You're a drunken slob. You're falling apart."

Raising her torso, breathing deep like an animal preparing to battle, she bared her yellow teeth. "You are a demon sent to me by order of Hell. I know how your kind thinks. I know your plans. And I won't be your pawn in any of it. I defy you demon from the North. I defy you. You want to kill me? Fine. I'll take your bitch with me and make you watch."

Sandra stepped forward and slapped Dr. Connor so hard that the woman fell to the ground. "For a witch, you sure are a fool. You were the killer, not us."

"Don't bother," Drummond said as he poked around the office. "She's out of her mind. Or just plain drunk."

"She has a book," Max said. "At least, she had one when I was last here."

"She's a witch. She has lots of books."

"This one's all about curses."

"I'll check on it." Drummond stepped through a wall deeper into the office.

With a garbled chuckle, the witch raised her head. "You want to know more about curses, eh? You want to know about a specific curse." Her eyes struck upon Max with an intensity unmatched by her slovenly appearance. Her youth returned to her eyes. "And a painting, I think."

Max's fears resumed their play on his nerves. "What do you know about Jasper Sullivan? How was he cursed?"

Still chuckling, Connor's eyes slipped away from Max and fell upon the half-empty Jack Daniel's bottle. She crawled over moldy pizza to the bottle and suckled it with wet, slobbering noises. With a relieved smile, she said, "I know all about that man and that painting. You may have ruined me, but I've still got contacts. I still have opportunities. Witches are like cats. Nine lives. You watch yourselves because I know everything you want to know."

"I'll bet you do. Your mother was the witch in charge back in William Hull's day, right?"

"Oh, yes. She was dangerous."

"And William Hull was angry that he had been duped on that painting. So he wanted her to hurt Jasper Sullivan in revenge."

"You sound like you know it all, but you don't."

Sandra leaned toward Max. "She's nuts. Let's just go."

Max squatted in front of Connor. He looked at her

expectant face and knew the time for payment had come. She had acknowledged that she knew something and, by sharing this fact, that she would be willing to tell it — but no witch does anything for free.

"Honey," he said without looking away from the witch. "Go to the ABC store and buy two, make it three, bottles of Jack Daniels." To Dr. Connor, he added, "Will that be enough?"

Connor swung her bottle upward and guzzled the remaining alcohol. "It just might."

She refused to say another word until Sandra returned. Drummond flew in, listened to what had happened, and said to Max, "You keep impressing me. If this were back in my time, we would've made a great team."

"We're barely partners."

"If I were alive, I'd make us a team, but I guess we do okay. I found the book back there. It's in pretty bad condition. Her private office is every bit as messed up as the rest of this place and keeping care of her books doesn't seem to have gotten any priority. Looks like she's been living back there for some time now."

"I'll look at it later. I don't want to leave her alone for any length of time."

Dr. Connor pointed at Max with a curved index finger that wavered in little arcs as she said, "Smart man. I still can do amazing things if I want to. Just takes a little focus and then that's it for you." She gazed in the vicinity of Drummond. "I know you're there, ghost. I feel you. I can still hurt you, too. Don't even think about touching me with your cold hands. I'll bind you back before you know I've even moved."

Drummond yawned. "Your wife better get back quick. I'm already tired of drunken witch-rantings."

Twenty minutes more passed before Sandra arrived with the whiskey. She handed the bottles to Max, gave the witch a vile glare, and stepped back near Drummond. Max handed one bottle over to Dr. Connor who broke open the seal with practiced efficiency and drank.

"Now," Max said, "if you want the rest of them, you'd

better start talking. Why was Jasper Sullivan cursed, what kind of curse, and how do we break it?"

"Don't forget the painting," Drummond said.

Max motioned for patience. Connor flashed her best insanity glower, and said, "You've got the whole thing wrong. Jasper Sullivan was never cursed. Executed, yes, but not cursed. After all, William Hull was not a bad man, not an unfair man. He understood why somebody like Sullivan would do what he did. This was the Great Depression. Times were hard and everybody needed money."

"Except Hull," Sandra said under her breath.

"Even the Hull family fell hard," Connor said, turning toward Sandra. "When the market goes bad, it goes bad for anybody with money. Now it's true that the Hulls did not suffer like a Sullivan or a Smith or even the Connor family — but they did have to go without many of the things they had become accustomed to." To Max, she continued, "William Hull would never order Jasper Sullivan to be cursed. But when they decided, in those uncertain times, to spend their money on a painting and then discovered they had lost their money and the painting both, well, Hull's anger could not be matched. Those responsible would have to pay. So, Jasper Sullivan ended up dead. Howard Corkille, however, became another matter entirely."

Max handed over another bottle. "Tell us all about it."

"I wasn't even born, remember. I only know what my mother told me when I took over the family business. It's important to keep track of curses and bindings and such. So she told me all about Howard Corkille in case I should ever have to deal with him or his curse. Very sad tale actually, but I suppose money will make people do sad things.

"In the case of Howard Corkille, he had done well as an art forger for almost a hundred years by the time he met Jasper Sullivan. Didn't know that, did you? It's true, though. Corkille was born in 1841. He was just over ninety when they met. I doubt he had done any forgeries in decades." Dr. Connor pulled more whiskey into her mouth, swished it around, and swallowed. "Whatever possessed him to help out Sullivan also brought back the thrill of screwing people over through his profession. Still, you'd think living around North Carolina for ninety years should've told him enough about the Hulls to dissuade him."

"So your mother bound him?"

With a snorting laugh, Dr. Connor stumbled to her feet and weaved her way down the hall toward her back office. Max and Sandra exchanged confused and curious looks as they followed the drunken witch. Drummond flew ahead through the wall.

The back office looked as if it had not been repaired since Max destroyed it over a year ago. The hole in the wall formed when he had broken her attempt at cursing him, the disheveled books and papers, the burned circle in the floor all flooded memories upon him — memories of the most harrowing time of his life. Max suspected she had brought them back here just for that reaction. The selfish amusement on her face supported this notion.

"You're very narrow-minded," she said, her speech clearing despite the bottle in her hand wetting her lips every few moments. "All three of you. You think that a binding curse is the only kind? You really think somebody who would employ a witch would be so uncreative in their choices of revenge?"

"You admire Hull," Sandra said.

"Of course, I do. The whole family is made of brilliant minds that don't fear the powers of life but accept them just because such things are — and they're willing to make use of it all. The trees, the sky, the water, the earth — all filled with great, untapped powers. Howard Corkille didn't understand any of that. He does now. All this time later, every day, he understands it. I'm sure Mr. Drummond understands it, too."

"Shut up," Drummond yelled as he soared at her. He slashed his hand through her body, and she let out a yelp. She shivered so hard, the bottle dropped from her hand and shattered. Then she began a long, sadistic cackle.

"Guess he doesn't like the truth too much," she said. "Shame I lost the bottle, though."

"Stick to Corkille," Max said, his eagerness for information the only thing keeping his distaste for this woman in check. "What kind of curse did your mother use?"

"She gave him immortality."

Max's eyebrow raised. "You can do that?"

"Do a little math — my mother was the Hull's witch during the Depression but I was born in 1973. She looked to be about thirty-five. If a spell can slow her aging, why not a spell to stop dying?"

"And this is a bad thing?"

"It is when you don't couple it with eternal youth. He's about two-hundred-years old now. I'd imagine every bone in his body aches. Food is tasteless. His eyesight, his hearing, even his sense of smell have all faded. Everyone he has known and cared about has grown old and died. But he is still here. Forever. I think that's quite cruel and imaginative."

Max's initial reaction leaned toward disbelief. But if ghosts, witches, and binding curses all were true, then why not immortality? Why not anything? The rules of the world he had been taught were wrong. Though he knew this to be true, he still struggled with it every day.

"Is this the curse?" Sandra asked. Max had not been paying close attention to her, and now saw her holding a thick, bound book — a book of curses.

Dr. Connor nodded without looking at the page. "There's only one in there that would match what I've said. You'll find it without any trouble."

Sandra flipped through the pages. Max watched her face reacting to the different words and images that passed under her gaze. Drummond, reading over her shoulder, jutted out his hand and said, "There. That's it."

"You're sure?" Max asked.

Sandra turned the book to face Max. Under some text he could not make out from that distance, he saw a clear, hand-drawn picture of a decrepit, old man — one who had to be centuries old. "We're sure," Sandra said.

Turning back to Connor and ignoring the snickers coming

from Drummond and Sandra, Max asked, "What does the painting have to do with this curse? Is it like the binding curse — attached to an object?"

"I'm done talking. No more," Connor said.

"You've got —"

"Out! Get out!" Waving her hands, she moved toward Sandra as if shooing cats away. "And take your ghost with you."

Sandra and Drummond backed out of the office. Dr. Connor turned to Max and with surprising speed, rushed close to him, her face so near his that he could smell her mouth washed in whiskey. Whispering in a hoarse voice, she said, "Come back here tonight, midnight, and I'll tell you exactly what you need to know about Hull. He's messing around with very dangerous magic, and we're all going to pay for it."

"Tell me now."

"Tonight. Midnight. The witching hour," she said and backed off with a sloppy, sinister grin.

# Chapter 12

"THIS IS A BAD IDEA," Drummond said as they left the office parking lot. "Whatever she wants to tell you is not worth meeting her at midnight."

"She could barely stand up."

"I don't care. A witch is not to be underestimated. If she had drunk herself into a coma, I'd still be worried."

Making a baby face, Max said, "Aw, are you worried about little ol' me?"

"On second thought, go get yourself killed."

"I promise I'll be careful. And the first part of that is being prepared. I think we should go visit with Melinda Corkille again. And this time around, I don't intend to leave without some answers."

"Good idea," Sandra said. "While you're doing that, Drummond can help me find that painting."

With a lecherous purr, Drummond said, "I love how you keep finding excuses for me to be with you."

"I need somebody who can go to the ghost world. You know any other ghosts that can help me, I'd be glad to work with them instead."

"If my heart were still beating, you'd have broken it."

"Wait a second," Max said. "I need you to come with me."

Sandra's odd expression told Max he teetered close to a fight. "You need me there?" she said, and even Drummond quieted down. "Every time you've gone there before, you refused to let me come along."

"Do we have to keep dredging this up? I made a mistake about that before, and I'm trying to do this the right way now. You understand?"

"You really just want to keep digging yourself deeper? No,

don't bother saying anything. We are either in this together, husband and wife, or we're not."

"What are you talking about?" Max said, exasperation painting every word.

"I've tried sitting back and letting you be the boss, but that's just not us. We don't rule over each other. So, while I appreciate your consideration, the fact is that I've got a few ideas on how we can find that painting. Going to Corkille's is a good idea. You can use her to locate — what is he? — her great-great-great grandfather? If the curse is real and he's still alive, you can find him. Drummond and I will get the painting, and you'll have all the leverage you need when you see that witch tonight. Now, if you've got a better plan, then I'll be happy to listen, but if you just want to boss me around ..."

"That's not fair," Max said. From the shocked look on Sandra's face and the echo in his ear, he realized too late that he had shouted the words. With a little more control, he went on, "I know I haven't done the best at any of this, I'm learning as I go, but you've got to cut me some slack here."

Shocked or not, Sandra plowed on. "Really? Cut you slack? What about me? I've been busting my ass in every way possible to help get this business going. How about a little appreciation?"

"This was a bad idea from the start." Max wanted to stop talking, wanted to rebuild the wall that crumbled around him, but he couldn't fight the momentum. The words kept spilling out of him. "If it weren't for your ability to see all the damn ghosts, you could be off doing something you really want to do instead of being stuck in my office all the time."

"That's it right there, isn't it? My ability. You want to play this off like it's all about me being around all the time, that I'm crowding you, but the truth is that you resent the fact that you need me. You hate it that without me, you don't have a business."

Drummond coughed and said, "I don't think I should be here now. I'll come back later."

"You stay still," Sandra said and Drummond obeyed.

"I'm trying to do right by us," Max went on, his face flushed and his brain trying to find a way out of this mess of an argument. "I screwed up in Michigan ... "

"You sure did."

" ... and I'm trying to make up for it. But having you scrutinize everything I do all day long isn't helping."

"I don't scrutinize."

"It sure feels that way."

Shaking his head more to himself than anyone else, Drummond floated between the couple. "Look, you two, we have a case to solve and a painting to find. That means time is a bit of a problem. So save the fight for when you're at home. We've got work to do."

"Fine with me," Sandra said. "Drummond and I have things to do."

"Fine," Max said. "I'll go see Melinda Corkille."

So, despite his decision never to do so, Max found himself in his car heading toward Melinda Corkille — alone.

The familiar drive performed its usual trick of pumping up Max's nerves. He already was fuming over fighting with his wife. But the closer he got to the Corkille house, the more his mind jumped from Dr. Connor and Terrance Hull to Sandra and Drummond, all the time dancing away from (yet sneaking glances at) memories of Melinda Corkille's naked back as she seductively stepped towards her bedroom. He had to calm down. A spat with the wife coupled with a seductress like Melinda only meant trouble. By the time he pulled into the Corkille's driveway, his hands were sore from tapping out every song the radio played.

She was out. Her car was gone, and a brown, dented Ford sat in its place — *Super-M Maids* printed on the side. Max blotted the back of his sleeve against his sweating forehead.

The front door to the house stood ajar while the sounds of vacuum cleaners and country music drifted outside. Max scanned the surrounding area — nobody watching. He hadn't trespassed since the Stan Bowman case last year, the same case that connected him to Hull and Connor and a whole mess of trouble. Max noted the irony as he stepped from the car and slinked toward the front door.

Though his heart pounded with adrenaline, a sense of relief washed over him. At least he had avoided meeting Melinda again. By comparison, this should be easy.

Standing in the open doorway, Max leaned in and listened. The twanging music came from his left — probably the kitchen. The vacuums whined away upstairs — not a place he wanted to visit. Most important of all, no sounds came from his right.

He took off his shoes and walked across the gleaming, hardwood floors in his socks. When he reached the room with the red sofa, he took a few gulps of air and looked around. Nothing appeared out of the ordinary. Just an average, filthy-rich living room. No desk, no papers, no bank statements.

"Of course not," he whispered. He could hear Drummond in his head — *This was the room she brought you to. Why would she let you spend time in a room with anything important in it?*

"But she's arrogant," he said. He bent over to look closer, going over the same pieces he had seen before — the same pictures, the same furniture, the same paintings, the same plants.

The door.

His head snapped up, and he stared at the narrow door with the plant in front of it. On his prior visit, he had assumed it was a broom closet. But she had him sit opposite the door, as if challenging him to see it, to ask about it.

*No. I'm just reading into this.* But what if ...

Making sure none of the maids were coming his way, he pulled the heavy plant to the side and opened the door. It led down a tiny hall and opened into an art studio — an art forger's studio.

In one way, the windowless room could have been an artist's studio. Canvases, paints, and brushes all had their special spots. An easel with a cloth-covered painting dominated the middle of the room. Two smocks hung on hooks to the side of the entrance, and several bulbs hung from the ceiling.

However, the room also looked unlike a typical artist's studio. On the wall opposite Max, he saw a utility sink next to a kitchen counter and a small refrigerator. On the counter were bread, a potato, coffee, tea, olive oil, gelatin, and flour. Max opened the fridge to find eggs and milk. A stove book-ended the counter and stacked on it was a pestle and mortar, two ice trays, a scale, some plates, detergent, and various papers and boards.

Max rummaged through the counter drawers. He found quills, numerous old pens, bottles of ancient inks, and sepia. One drawer had been filled with brushes stained in ink, charcoal, chalk, and other dried mediums.

And the key detail, the one Max knew he noticed only from spending time learning from Drummond — no dust. This art forging studio was still being used. It was possible Melinda had followed in Howard's footsteps, but that did not seem likely. Melinda came off as too selfish to apply herself to the years of study required for such a thing. Of course, the alternative had yet to penetrate Max fully. He knew curses and witches were real, but to accept that somewhere in this mansion rested a two-hundred-year-old criminal, pushed Max's sense of the world further than it had ever gone before.

"Only one way to be sure."

Max slipped his shoes back on and walked into the kitchen. He made sure to use heavy steps, the kind that echoed throughout such a large house. One maid, a blonde girl no more than eighteen, stood on a stepstool and scrubbed at food caked across the inner face of a microwave. When she saw Max, she stepped down and wiped her hands.

"Excuse me," Max said with a disarming smile.

"Who are you?" the girl asked, lacking all the Southern friendliness he had come to know.

"I'm sorry," he said, and put out his hand. "I'm Trevor Denton." He had no clue where that name came from but did not question himself either. "I'm Ms. Corkille's personal assistant."

"What happened to Jenine?"

"She still works for Ms. Corkille, too. I've just been brought in to help out with a few things. It's a busy time right now."

Still cautious but softening a little, the maid said, "Oh. Okay, so what do you want?"

"Ms. Corkille asked for some papers but this is my first time in her house, and well, it's big."

The girl laughed. "Yeah. It took me a few times before I figured the whole thing out."

"I imagine so. But I'm pressed for time. I've got to get the papers to the courthouse today or Ms. Corkille will be very angry."

The girl blanched. Nobody wanted to see Ms. Corkille angry. "I can show you her office."

Up until this point, his bluff had been quite easy. With what little he knew, the maid seemed willing to believe just about any basic idea. The problem was now. Where would Melinda be hiding Howard? "No," he said on instinct. "She said they were in a different room."

"Which room? There are quite a few."

Which one, indeed? Howard Corkille would not be hidden in any common room or any room that the maids were expected to clean. "She wasn't too clear," Max finally said. "It sounded like she was driving when she called me. She told me it was another room but it wasn't one with a name like kitchen or bathroom or anything like that. Is she always like this?"

With a conspiratorial wink, she said, "Not always. Just most of the time."

"Because the last person I was an assistant for drove me nuts with these half-explained requests. I mean, what am I supposed to do? Go through every room in this mansion?"

"What kind of papers are these?"

"I don't know. They're in an envelope. Just get them to the courthouse. That's all I know."

"I wonder if she meant the Other Room."

"What's that?"

"Just a third guest room but she never wants it cleaned or even opened. We call it the Other Room because sometimes you hear things moving in there. If I believed in ghosts, I'd say that room was haunted. But, of course, that kind of thing is silly."

"Of course," Max said with a knowing smile.

"You better call her before you go in there, though. She's very strict about it."

"Thank you. I'll do that. Where is this room?"

"Upstairs at the end of the hall."

"Thanks again."

The maid offered her first flash of warmth — a slight curve of the lips.

Max found a set of servants' stairs from the kitchen and climbed up. He walked along the wide hall and listened to the upstairs maids working. They were in a bedroom on the left, and Max did not stop when he passed by. They either didn't notice him or didn't care. He was happy enough whichever way it was.

As he neared the end of the hall, his nerves reignited. The Other Room awaited just beyond a dark, wooden door. If he took too long, the maids might wonder about him — What's with the guy standing in front of the Other Room? That might lead to questions and then the whole thing would blow up. No, he had to do this now.

He opened the door and stepped in.

The Other Room was another guest room — enough space to place a twin bed, a bedside table, and a small chest of drawers on the side. One window spread sunlight into the dingy interior. The walls were covered in wallpaper from another era, brown vertical designs that hid dirt better than brighten the room. In the back corner, a Japanese tri-fold screen stood with a delicate painting of two birds on a ghostly limb. At the foot of the bed, a rocking chair faced the window. Max saw a man sitting in the chair.

"Mr. Corkille?" he said, his voice distant and inconsequential. "Howard Corkille?"

The rocking stopped and a single hand emerged from the side to gesture Max closer. When Max obliged, he saw a man hunched over, covered in wrinkles and age spots, destroyed by a lifetime over a century too long. The man peered up and grinned.

"Nice to see a different face," he said. He spoke with a sickening crackle that underscored every word.

Max's muscles refused to move. The man sitting before him frightened him as if he looked upon the living dead — not a rotting zombie from the movies, but rather a warm, fully fleshed but decrepit human being. Max feared to shake the offered hand, feared it might crumble in his grip.

Perhaps reading Max's expression, Corkille said, "Don't worry. You can't hurt me. Nothing can."

"The curse?" Max said, shaking the coarse, dried hand lightly.

"Oh, yes. I didn't believe in magic and curses and such until I tangled with the Hull family. Now, I know. When I was first put under this curse, I tried to prove it wasn't true." Corkille pulled back his sleeve to show long scars stretching from the crook of his arm to his wrist. "The skin would just seal back up. I once bought a shotgun and thought to blow my head off. It jammed. Every time I pointed it at myself, it jammed. Point it at the wall, no problem." Corkille gestured to the scattered holes in the wall. "Point it at myself — click."

"I can't imagine."

"After a while, I stopped trying. Then I just got older and older. My body got weaker. My eyesight's remained. Thank the Lord for that. My hearing sucks. I smell horrible. Bladder control went out ninety years ago. Everything's failing little by little. But my mind won't ever go. Curses work that way, y'see. It won't let me have the pleasure of escaping any of this through dementia. I have to experience it every step. And I'm tired. I just want to die, just close my eyes and sleep forever."

When Corkille closed his eyes, Max thought he might fall asleep. He thought he had to keep Corkille talking, but with his next question, he found that Corkille was eager to talk with anybody. Isolation can have that effect.

"And you need the painting?" Max asked.

Corkille looked at his hands. "Painting was my life. I loved it since I was a boy. I remember an artist traveling through town, stopping wherever to do portraits to make a little money — that's when it all started for me. He gave me a brush and he taught me a bit. I caught the bug.

"My father was dead and my mother, she supported me. We worked hard to pull together enough money to get me schooled. And I learned to paint.

"I suppose some psychiatrist would blame it on being raised poor, would say that's why I took to forging. Maybe it's a little true. I certainly was attracted to the money and to thumbing my nose at the art world — they can be such asses. I don't know if this is true for all criminals, but for some of us, for me, there was an attraction to breaking laws. Not that I wanted to go hurting people but that I discovered a sense of freedom, a sense of invulnerability, that I've never found at any other time in my life.

"Felt it right up until the moment that witch came along and laid a curse upon me. But then, you know all about this kind of thing."

Through deadening eyes, Corkille stared straight at Max. Max fought the urge to flee. "What do you mean?"

"No need to play games, Mr. Porter."

"You know who I am?"

Corkille cracked a sly grin that could have belonged to Melinda. "Do you think you're the only one who does research? I was cursed by a witch that worked for the Hull family. I pay attention to anything involving those two."

"You've been watching me."

"Not me personally. I'm too old for that. But, yes, since you first moved down here. That whole business with Stan Bowman and the Drummond curse — I followed you through every step. You handled yourself well, and I thought even back then that if I needed your type of services, I wouldn't hesitate to call. And now I need you."

Max shook his head. "Wait. You didn't call me. I found you. You've been hiding out all this time, not trying to contact me."

"True, I did not try to contact you. Not true, that I've just been hiding out here. I've been searching for that painting for many years."

"What's so important about it?"

"This is dangerous. I had hoped to avoid involving you, and I feared doing so would gain the attentions of Hull or the witch, but it seems they already are paying attention. So, now that we're talking, now that I've met you in person, I think you are the perfect man to find that painting."

Max leaned against the window frame with an exasperated sigh. "Really? I'm *the perfect man?* Is this a joke? No one will even tell me why some painting that has no apparent value is so important. And I'm perfect. So, why do you want it?"

"To help break this curse, of course. Surely, by now, you've come to understand that much. Why else would a witch be involved if not for magic? Why else would an occultist like Hull care so much? Listen, I will pay you double your fee, and I promise that when you find me that painting, you'll have plenty more."

The bedroom door burst open. "What the hell are you doing in here?" Melinda Corkille said, her face taut and red.

Max stammered but Howard turned towards her, raised his hands in celebration, and said, "My dear, we've just hired Mr. Porter."

# Chapter 13

WHEN MAX WALKED INTO HIS OFFICE, Sandra and Drummond turned, ready to launch into whatever business they wanted to share. One look at his stunned face stopped them. As he explained what happened since they had argued, their faces also dropped into shock.

After Max finished, nobody said a word. The only sound was the droning buzz of a fan Sandra had set on her desk. Drummond was the first to break the silence. "So, we're working for Corkille now?"

"I think so," Max said. "I think his side of this story is the most honest."

"You know he's lying about something, though, right?"

"Don't they always?"

Drummond clapped his hands. "There you go. That's what I like. Healthy skepticism. I can see now that I'm doing a bang-up job. Teaching you perfectly."

"I guess," Sandra said, "it's time for me to earn my keep."

Max shook his head. "Can we not start in on that fight right now?"

"I wasn't being sarcastic. And considering all of this Corkille stuff, I think you'll be very happy with what I have to say."

"Hey," Drummond said. "I was part of this, too."

"I haven't forgotten."

"One of you tell me," Max said.

Sandra puffed up a little. "I think we've found the painting."

Until he heard those words from his wife's lovely lips, Max didn't think his day could get any weirder. So many questions flooded his brain that he shut down, staring stupefied at his wife. The ghost behind her spoke first.

"I'm the one who figured out the name change."

Max snapped to. "What name change?"

Drummond slid into his chair, kicked up his feet, and said, "I've been spending a lot of time with ghosts lately, trying to find out whatever I can about Corkille and Sullivan and everything else. A lot of them, not all ghosts, but a lot of them moan and groan about the lives they had. Just a bunch of pansies. And they cry on about how many people came to their funerals and who said what and so forth. I was trying to have a pleasant conversation with this figure skater who cracked her neck on the ice, poor thing was only twenty-three, beautiful gal who had a promising career. Great mouth, too. Smile that just melted me."

"The point, please."

"Oh, right. Anyway, we were just talking and I was about to lay a good line on her, the kind that would've led to a date without a doubt, when this old lady floats by wailing and wailing about being dead. I lost it. You know, sometimes these things just build up inside you and her little tirade set me off. I yelled at her. And she turned to me with such hatred and self-pity and she said, 'I'm sure you had a wonderful funeral with plenty of people to cry for you, but not me. I was a good person and only three mourners came. Just three.' She yapped on, but I didn't hear any of it. Because it hit me just then — what if the painting was actually called 'Mourning in Red,' as in at a funeral?"

Sandra flitted about with sudden energy like an excited schoolgirl. "When Drummond told me about his idea, I just knew he was right. We did some searches but came up empty. Then we tried some of the art dealer forums, and guess who we found to be looking for the same painting?"

Max looked at the floor. "Gold," he said as if he could shoot the name into the art gallery below.

"Bingo. But it doesn't look like he's had any success."

Drummond said, "Gold's not looking under the right name. He's still just an idiot."

Sandra continued, "The name is a big part of it, but then I realized that we were searching the wrong way. This painting is not a valuable painting. The artist isn't well-known. Nothing we've been told indicates that anybody not involved with this whole curse even knows the painting exists. It's not a famous painting. It's common. So, we should go where we little common folk go."

"First, we checked eBay," Drummond said with a twinkle of pride at using computer lingo, "but nobody had listed it."

"This is my part of the story," Sandra said.

"Sorry."

"Next we went to craigslist, and again we found nothing. And then I decided to post on craigslist myself. I simply named the painting and how much I'd pay for it. Don't worry, not much — but then, it isn't worth that much to most people."

"And we got a hit."

"Drummond!"

"I'm sorry, but I'm just as happy as you are."

Max waved off their little spat. "You got a hit? Where? When? Heck, who?"

Sandra said, "A guy named Chris Thorne, and he lives just north of us in Virginia. We only need to set up a time and place to exchange for the painting."

"Don't you usually send a check and get it in the mail?"

"Do you really want to risk it that way, or do the whole thing in person?"

"I guess we're taking a little trip to Virginia. When do we go?"

"He should e-mail me tonight."

"Great," Max said. "You've both done a great job."

Sandra kissed Max on the cheek. "Since we can't do anything about the painting until we get the e-mail, why don't we do a bit of premature celebration. Care for an early dinner and some alcohol? I think we could both use it."

"Hey," Drummond said. "That's not very fair to me."

Sandra rolled out her bottom lip. "So sorry. But there's not much we can actually do for you, is there?"

"You could quit mocking me. And you don't have to rub it in all the time. I know I'm a ghost."

Max put his arm around Sandra's shoulder. He knew things were not suddenly okay between them, and he knew she was aware of it, too. But one thing he had learned through the course of their marriage — some days it paid more to let the ugly stuff slide away for a while. To Drummond, he said, "We'll be back later to check on that e-mail."

Dinner was a pleasant affair. They went to Fourth Street and enjoyed the Italian wonders of Dioli's Trattoria. Despite the shadow of the witch's impending midnight meeting looming over him, Max managed to push fear away long enough to eat. He drank in the beauty of his wife and the joy of her success, and he felt capable of facing the witch. If all went well, within the next day or two, he would have that painting, this case would be over, he'd get paid, and life would become easier. If.

By the time he wiped cannoli crumbs from his mouth, the fears had resurfaced. Sandra knew, of course — she took one look at his troubled face and he saw her understanding. He shook his head, and she stayed quiet.

They went home, watched some nonsense on television, and when it was time that they normally would get dressed for bed, Max donned his coat. This time, however, Sandra did not stay quiet. "I'm coming with you," she said, and Max knew better than to argue. Besides, if he was honest with himself, he wanted her along.

Twenty minutes later, they sat in their car across the street from the witch's office. "It was about a year ago that we were sitting here like this," Max said.

"Yeah," Sandra said. "This time feels worse."

Max watched the digital clock in his car stereo add another minute. "Yeah," he whispered. With only two minutes until midnight, Max stepped out of the car. The 'door ajar' bell chimed repeatedly, its sharp tone standing out in the quiet night air.

"How long should I wait?" Sandra asked.

"Until I either come out or you hear me screaming."

"That's not funny."

"Wasn't meant to be," he said and walked toward the office.

It never got easier — crossing that small parking lot in the dead of night. He had done this several times, and each instance twisted his nerves into a ball of wriggling worms. He hated the witch's office — hated that he never knew what he would find when he opened the door.

The cool night air prickled his skin, and when he reached the overhang, he wondered if he might be better off turning around and leaving. Yes, the witch promised important information, but she had done terrible things before — cursing him would be the least of her sins. Still, the desperation in her eyes that morning led Max to believe that this was no trap. The question that plagued him, though, was *What exactly is this?*

The door was unlocked. Max touched the knob, his fingers trembling over the rusting metal, and pushed the door in.

The darkness in the waiting room neared pitch black. If not for the lone candle at the far end of the hall, Max would have seen nothing. But she wanted him to see a little bit. That much was clear. She had left a blatant marker, and as Max headed down the hall, as his gut tightened around the remnants of dinner, he considered that the drunken soul he had seen that morning might have been acting.

When he reached the candle, he smelled incense burning from the closed office door. "Come in," Dr. Connor called.

*Last chance,* he thought, looking back down the hall.

But the office door opened, and Dr. Connor stood before him wearing a black gown and looking more in control of herself. Four clusters of candles lit the room, one cluster at the mid-point of each wall. They cast competing shadows behind her as she stepped back and gestured to one of the two chairs facing each other in the center.

"You seem much better than this morning," Max said as he leaned against the entryway. The warmth of the candles pressing against him matched the pain in his stomach pushing to get out.

"I was not at my best," she said with a fluttering chuckle.

"But I want to thank you. You've given me a little ray of hope, and that has made me feel much, much better."

"I did?"

"Only fitting since you were the one who destroyed me."

The ice in her voice struck out at Max, reminding him that no matter what, this woman should only be seen as dangerous. "What do you want?" he asked.

"Information, of course. Isn't that what you trade in?"

"I don't have anything for you."

"You definitely do. And in exchange, as promised, I will tell you what Terrance Hull is doing and why it is vital to you and your interests."

Despite his pounding heart, Max acted as if none of this mattered. "Fine. You go first."

Dr. Connor licked her lips and said, "Please, sit down." With a sweeping motion, she went to her desk and reached underneath. A string quartet piped in from ceiling speakers. Max didn't recognize the piece but it was a somber, slightly dissonant sound that made the witch appear more devious, more of a threat.

*Exactly what she wants.*

"Come now," she said, stepping toward the chairs. "I promise I won't curse you tonight."

"How comforting."

The idea of heading further into this spider's web did not appeal to Max, but he wanted to hear what she had to say. There were so many loose threads, and if this witch would tie some of it together, even just one or two things, he had to take a few chances. No risk, no reward — Drummond would be proud.

When Max settled into his chair. Connor sat opposite him. "I'm sure Howard Corkille has told you his pathetic little story. He probably even told you some of the truth. But what you should know is that Terrance Hull is not seeking the painting as some sort of retribution upon Corkille for deceiving his grandfather. He never even liked the old man that much. No, Terrance Hull needs to find the painting for the same reason he needed to get his journal back a year ago. They are two of three key charms to a powerful spell. I was to cast that spell, but because of you, Hull is not as confident in me as he once was. When you help me get this painting back to him," she said, her eyes turned toward the ceiling as if peering into the future, "he will care about me again."

"So, what's this spell?"

"Simply to raise Tucker Hull back from the grave with more power than he ever had when alive, to restore him to his place as the head of the Hull family, but this time, with an enormous fortune to wield."

"Is that all?"

Dr. Connor curled her lip. "For now."

"And you actually think I'll help you do this?"

She placed her middle finger on Max's forehead and slid it down to the tip of his nose. "You will be eager to help me."

Max swore she kept speaking, but he could not hear anything. A weight pressed into his body as if a sandbag had been dumped into his lap. At first, he thought it was fear taking over. As Dr. Connor edged back, concentrating on him and mouthing silent words, he knew the weight was not fear but some kind of spell.

"Stop this." He tried to lift his arms but they wouldn't budge from his side.

"I just need to ensure that you won't do anything rash."

"I'm not going to help you," he said, while a voice deep inside questioned his timing for bravado.

"I wonder what your wife will say about it?"

"What?"

"She must be feeling a bit lonely outside, in that cold car, waiting for you to play your little detective game with me. She must be wishing something more exciting would happen."

Max strained against his invisible bonds. Though he knew she would never hear him, Max screamed Sandra's name, begged her to drive away — even as he pictured Dr. Connor's hired hands ripping open the car door and yanking her out. She would struggle. She would fight back with a kick or a punch, but they would overpower her.

The witch had his wife.

Dr. Connor sauntered to her rolltop desk and opened the half-empty bottle of Jack Daniel's. She tipped back her head and guzzled for a moment. With a satisfied exhalation, she returned to Max. "Now," she said, "you will help me get that painting, so that I may return to Terrance's favor. If you don't, I'm sure the Hulls will always have need for a good blood sacrifice."

With the coldest, most hateful scorn he ever held, Max nodded. He thought to threaten her should anything happen to Sandra, but he could see in her eyes that she knew. And though Drummond was not in the room, Max could hear his strong voice saying, "There's no way this is going to end up good."

# Chapter 14

MAX SLAMMED OPEN HIS OFFICE DOOR, cracking the glass right across the gold-painted 319, and headed straight for the bookshelf. He grabbed the first book he could reach, opened it, found only pages, and tossed it aside. Another book. Another. And another.

Drummond entered from the ceiling and said, "Um, Max? You feeling okay?"

"What does it look like?" He tilted three books from the shelf and watched them fall to the floor.

"Take it easy. Those are my books."

"You got a gun here and I want it."

"I don't have a gun."

Max grabbed the well-used book that hid Drummond's whiskey bottle. "You got this. And I don't believe at all that you ever went around without a gun when you were alive. So, where is it?"

"Calm down."

"Get me the fucking gun!"

"I swear I don't have one."

Max scanned the room until his eyes rested on the floor. "Of course," he said, and stomped on the floorboards. "Which one is it? Tell me."

"I don't—"

"Damn it!" Max said, hammering his desk with his fist. "They've got Sandra. You understand that? That witch took her from me. So, you tell me where that gun is. I've got to get her back."

Despite the pain of corporeal contact, Drummond concentrated enough to push a chair closer to Max. "Tell me what happened."

Max stared at the chair, his hands itching to rip up the floor, but finally lowered his head with a sigh. He pulled the whiskey from the book and drank. Then he told everything as best as he could remember. Twice he had to stop for another swig. He hoped Drummond would cut him off and reveal the location of a gun, but the ghost only listened until the telling finished.

"This is bad," Drummond said.

"Now you know. Please, where's the gun?"

"What do you think you're going to do? Go blazing into Hull family headquarters and demand Sandra back or you'll start shooting?"

Sheepish, Max said, "Something like that."

"No." The timbre of Drummond's voice caught Max's attention — filled with sorrow and shock. Drummond closed in on Max, his body lacking the usual grace of a ghost and instead moving like he felt every year since his death attacking each muscle. He was worried. That worried Max more. "I've dealt with things like this before," Drummond said. "And we've both dealt with Hull. You know you can't just go running in there. You'll only get her killed and probably yourself, too."

"I can't just sit here."

"You need to get control of yourself so we can plan. Now, you said they want you to find the painting, right?"

"Yeah."

"Well, we have found it. Let's see if our seller wrote back to Sandra. If we're lucky, we can get that painting fast, and then we'll have something of value to them."

An e-mail awaited them on Sandra's computer (Max felt weird using her property as if he was already stepping toward the acknowledgement that she might no longer need such things) — the seller wanted to do the transaction by mail. Max wrote back that the painting was meant as a gift, so he needed it right away. The seller replied that for a few extra dollars, he'd use overnight shipping.

"We can't do that," Drummond said. Max agreed. It was too easy to see Hull somehow intercepting the package.

Drummond clapped his hands at a new idea. "Tell him that

we'll pay an extra fifty percent if he'll meet us tomorrow."

"In case you forgot, we don't have any money."

"It's going on a credit card, isn't it?"

Max kicked the desk. Then he wrote the offer. The seller agreed to meet at the North Carolina Welcome Center off Route 77, but he wanted to meet right away.

"He thinks we're doing something illegal," Drummond said. "Could work to our advantage. Meet him at two a.m. It'll give you time to get ready but it's so early that he'll still feel secretive about it. That's good for us."

Max wrote back and the deal was set.

"Get some rest," Drummond said when Max turned off the computer. "You'll be on the road in a few hours. I'll come as far as I can, but I suspect the border is a bit longer than my leash will allow."

Max threw back a last shot of whiskey, barely feeling the burn in his throat, and propped his feet up on the desk. *Just like an old detective,* he thought, picturing Drummond back in the 1940s. It almost felt good. But with Sandra in such danger, good feelings, like sleep, would not come.

The Welcome Center had always struck Max as more than a glorified rest stop. Situated on the slope of a mountain, Highway 77 barely audible from the distance thanks to copious trees, the place reminded Max of a lovely park. In fact, were it closer to home, he might have considered it a nice place for a picnic, though the terraced land had been designated mostly for parking. At the top of a series of stairways, the open building sat providing bathrooms to weary travelers.

Max stood by his car and watched as the few people on the road this late at night stretched and walked. The lot below rumbled with the sounds of numerous trucks — most set up for the driver to sleep for a few hours. A heavyset man paced at the top of the stairs leading to the bathrooms.

Max waited as two groups of travelers arrived, used the facilities and left. For the moment, the Welcome Center was empty except for Max and the heavyset man who still paced atop the stairs. With a final scan of the area — too dark to make out much at all — Max climbed the stairs.

"You Max?" the man asked.

Max nodded. "Where's the painting?"

"In my truck. Come on."

The man wore a yellow windbreaker that made an odd shushing sound as he walked. He checked out Max a few times, bashful when caught, and wiped his hands on his coat several times. Max glanced around as they walked.

Nothing in this man's behavior signaled a threat. If anything, the guy struck Max as somebody who came upon the painting and now hoped to make a quick buck selling it. The late-night exchange made the guy nervous but not enough to turn down the cash. And since no matter how many times he looked, Max didn't notice any danger, he felt better about the situation.

They approached a rusty Ford pickup, and the man said, "Y'know, we've had this painting for years. Just catching dust in the shed. I would never have found your ad 'til my brother phoned me up. You suppose it's worth something?"

"Not really," Max said. "It's not famous or anything. Just an old family painting that got sold off long ago by accident. In fact, we always thought we had it until my grandfather died and we learned that it was gone. That's why we put out the ad." Drummond would be amazed at how smoothly the story slipped off his tongue.

The man nodded with regret as if to say that things always turned out this way for him. He pulled out a smartphone to run Max's credit card. "Well, I can't say I don't wish it were something worth millions but I'll take what I can get."

"Millions would be nice, wouldn't it?"

The man laughed, a big rosy-faced grin, and then his lips formed a small O. A little red trail leaked from his hairline. Only when the man's eyes rolled up did Max's brain register the sound of a gunshot. The man dropped to the ground dead, and Max dropped, too. His mind raced to catch up with events.

The gunshot had sounded far off. A sniper? And the bullet

had struck the man somewhere on the side of the head — which meant Max had no real cover at the moment. As if to illustrate the point, a bullet shot through the side of the truck just above his head.

Max rolled underneath the truck and shimmied behind the dead man's body. Now he had cover — for the moment. He was impressed with himself for not panicking and for acting with some thought. Not too long ago, he probably would have ended up dead. Now, at least, he had a chance. Except waiting to be shot again while congratulating himself wasn't going to save his life. He cleared his mind and focused on the present.

He needed to get out of there, get to his car, get to safety. But he needed that painting, too. Without that, Sandra had no hope.

Max reached forward and patted the man's pants. *Stop being a tentative prick and get the keys.* He shoved his hand down the pockets nearest him. Neither one had a key. With a deep breath, he reached over the body and fumbled for the far pocket.

Another shot popped into the truck above. Max's hands shook but he worked for the pocket as best he could. Trying to keep some cover, his face buried into the lifeless man's stomach. The man smelled of aftershave and alcohol — not a bad scent but a combination Max hoped never to smell again.

He felt a wallet but no keys. Another gunshot popped in the distance, and the dead man took a bullet in the shoulder. Max jumped at the hit, smacking his head against the underside of the truck. He hurried back underneath, rubbing his head. That's when he heard the jingle of keys.

Without exposing himself to the sniper, Max placed his foot on the dead man and gave a soft push. Again, the jingle of keys. Not a pants pocket, then, but a jacket pocket.

He rolled closer to the body and reached into the near-side jacket pocket. With closed eyes and a silent prayer that he wouldn't have to go over the body to the other side pocket, his finger felt around. And he found it. A ring with five keys.

He snatched the keys free, rolled to the passenger side of the truck, and crouched beneath the door. One by one he tried the keys. The first two wouldn't go in. The next three went in but wouldn't turn the door. Before he let despair take over, though, he heard Drummond in the back of his head — "You're nervous. Try again."

The first key failed, but the second key actually slipped in and turned. Max opened the door. In the back of the cab, behind the passenger seat, he found a painting wrapped in brown paper. It wasn't large — all of two feet long and a foot-and-a-half wide. He pulled it from the cab and crouched back down.

His pulse hammered as he clutched the painting. He kept expecting a shot to hit him. But the sniper hadn't done anything for the last few moments. Why? "He's a sniper," Max told himself, his words coming out in shaky breaths. "He's going to reposition."

Max looked down at the brown-wrapped painting. An idea popped into his mind. Without debating himself, he dashed across the parking lot with his body in a low crouch like soldiers did in the movies — and he held the painting like a shield. Whoever hired this gunman to kill him wanted the painting. Anybody willing to kill for a painting wants it undamaged — no excuses. As long as Max didn't provide a clear target, as long as the sniper risked hitting the painting, he would be safe. At least, that's what he hoped for.

When he reached the stairs, the thought that he might survive sparked. He turned toward his car, putting the painting behind him, and scurried to the driver's side. Two shots snapped the asphalt at his feet. Max didn't stop. He couldn't — his body refused to do anything but keep running for the car.

He wrenched the door opened with a screech and jumped in. Tossing the painting to the side, he shoved his keys into the ignition. He kept his head low as he started the car and turned on the brights. The entire Welcome Center lot became washed in the strong car lights. Peeking over the dashboard, he searched for any movement, any sign of his attacker.

Though the restrooms were uphill and covered with trees,

Max swore he glimpsed a thin, blond-haired man dashing off. He waited and watched. Nobody came out.

He slipped the car into drive, and with his body hunched over the wheel, he tore off onto the highway. A mile passed by before he would sit up straight. Another mile passed before he slowed down enough to stop the car from shaking.

Now only he was shaking.

# Chapter 15

BY THE TIME HE ARRIVED at Melinda Corkille's home, Max's head had entered that late-night fuzziness. His dashboard clock read 2:57 am and he felt every second of sleep deprivation dancing along his skin. When he rang the doorbell and knocked on the wood, the sounds echoed in his ears.

Several minutes later, the porch light winked on and the door opened. Melinda poked her groggy face outside and squinted. "What the hell are you doing here?"

"I've got it," he said and pushed his way in. "Get Howard."

Melinda's mouth tightened into a firm line. "I am not waking up that man in the middle of the night for anything."

"You don't understand."

"Go home, Max. I'll call the police if I have to. And I don't care what Howard said before. He is not getting worked up into all this just to have you ditch him in the end. I've seen it before. Idiots come along intrigued by his story and they want to help him break the curse. Only thing that gets broken is him."

"But I've got the painting. *Mourning in Red* — I've got it."

Melinda stood dumbfounded. As her thoughts finally connected, she stammered a few syllables and finally managed, "I-I'll get Howard."

"Thank you," Max said with a sarcastic bow.

While she left the room, Max hurried back to his car to retrieve the painting. He paused at the door, his eyes searching the darkness, his heart pressing against his chest. Just because he got away doesn't mean the sniper gave up.

"I'm not giving up, either." He pictured Sandra, tried to will his good thoughts toward her, and then set about his work.

When he returned to the house, Melinda was escorting

Howard to his art studio. Max hadn't noticed her when he had first arrived — he just wanted to get to Howard — but seeing Melinda in a silk robe and a revealing piece of flimsiness underneath caused his pulse to quicken in a different manner than before. But that was just testosterone doing its thing. He closed his eyes, pictured Sandra once more, and focused on what was important.

Melinda waved him in. Max could see the excitement on Howard's face. With care, he set the painting on one of Howard's easels and stepped back.

"It's still wrapped," Melinda said.

Max nodded. "I didn't want to take anything away from Howard." As much as he felt the clock ticking against him, Max did find the resolve to let Howard have his moment.

Howard lifted a shaking hand to the painting. His bony fingers found a small nick, and with surprising strength, he ripped off the brown-paper wrapping. Melinda helped remove the remaining strips.

All three stared at the sad painting. It portrayed a voluptuous, nude woman posed on a red couch with her left hand covering between her legs. Her right hand pressed against her brow creating a shadow over her closed eyes that only accentuated the deep sadness she clearly felt.

"Is this the right painting? I thought it was supposed to be a landscape."

Howard's unsteady finger traced the bumps of paint, getting stronger as he moved along the canvas. "This is the right one."

"You painted this?" Melinda asked.

Corkille's mouth twisted like a disapproving teacher. He reached for a bottle on his desk, soaked a rag with its contents, and wiped it on the painting. With only three broad strokes, the paint smeared off.

"Stop him!" Max said. Each wipe felt like a strike against Sandra.

Melinda put her hand on Howard's shoulder but he threw it off. "No," he said. "Watch close."

A few more strokes of the rag and they all saw what Howard

wanted them to see — underneath the paint was another painting.

"I don't believe it," Max said. "What the hell is that?"

"That," Howard said, working off more paint with a gentle touch, "is what we all are after."

The second painting, the real painting, sent tremors along Max's nerves. It showed a dark figure, a huge man, standing in a doorway. Little wisps of smoke snaked from either side of his head. The doorway overlooked a room without any defined end. Strange symbols, the kind Dr. Connor used, floated around another nude figure — Max couldn't tell the sex because the figure was curled into a ball.

Melinda's face brightened. "Can this do it? Can this really help you break the curse?"

"Of course," Howard said.

Max put a hand on the edge of the painting. "Then break your curse now. I need to take this painting."

Melinda shot to her feet so fast she startled Howard. "Don't you dare."

"This isn't the way I want it, but I don't have a choice."

"Was this the point all along? Just use Howard like everybody always did?"

"They have my wife. Sandra. They have her, and the only leverage I've got is that painting."

"Well you'll have to find something else. This poor man here has suffered long enough. He needs this painting, and that's it."

"We're talking about the witch, Connor," Max said, his voice breaking.

In a grim tone, Howard said, "And that means the Hull family, too."

"I don't know. Probably. I haven't thought it out that far. All I know is Connor and her thugs have my wife. They'll kill her. Or worse."

Melinda sat back with Howard and rested her head on his shoulder, leaving Max standing alone and feeling a thousand miles away from that painting and even further from Sandra.

Tears welled in his eyes. His lungs didn't want to breath in. Everything inside his body wanted to shut down.

"Please," he whispered.

Melinda didn't answer him, and Howard continued to run his fingers over the painting. Max could hear what Drummond would say, and a trace of his usual fiery passion simmered deep inside, but he stayed still. His mind conjured images long forgotten.

He remembered the final days of his grandmother. She had outlived all her friends. She had lost her hearing years before and her sight amounted to fuzzy blobs of light and dark. Her bones were brittle and her muscles weak. At ninety-four years old, she had been reduced to spending her days sitting on the balcony of her nursing home and barely noticing the world drift by.

At ninety-four.

Howard had surpassed that age by over a century. Though he was in better health, that wasn't saying a lot. And as he got older, his body would get worse. Eventually, he would be just as broken, just as empty. Then he had eternity to look forward to. As much as Max wanted to snatch that painting and run to Hull, to Sandra, a part of him couldn't deny this ancient man a release from immortality.

"Okay," Max said. "You tell me what needs to be done with this painting to break the curse, and I'll do it. Afterward, whatever is left, give it to me. Let me save Sandra."

Howard looked up as if he had just become aware of the others around him. "No. You must help your wife now."

Melinda sputtered. "W-What? But the curse —"

"I'll get rid of the curse. Don't worry. But I don't need the painting itself. This is not a sacred object. It's really more of a map. And once I decipher it, then I'll know where to go to find what I do need."

"A map? To what?"

Howard grinned and Max's bones chilled. "To one of the most powerful bits of magic I ever heard about."

Melinda rubbed her temples. "Fine. Okay. Then we still

need the painting, even if it's the only map."

With his hand shaking again, Howard pointed to the living room. "Get your purse." Melinda complied, and Howard said, "You have a phone that takes pictures, right? Take one of the whole painting. Then form a nine-square grid in your mind like a tic-tac-toe board, and take several pictures of each square — one of each square must be as close to the canvas as you can get, so I can see the textures. When you finish, give Max the painting and I'll get started."

As Melinda took the photos, Max asked, "You're going to forge this painting?"

"That's what I'm best at."

Melinda left the room to download and print out the photos. Max sat next to Howard and stared at the dark painting. "Are you sure you don't need the original?"

Howard patted Max's knee. "Even if I did need it, I've long outlived my selfishness. No way could I let Hull's witch curse or kill your wife. But don't worry. I'm not lying to you and Melinda. As long as I can reproduce this painting — and I can — then I should be able to find what I need."

Max picked up Howard's hand and looked the old man straight in the eyes. "When I get Sandra safe, you have my word. I'll come back here. I'll help you."

With a gritty chuckle, Howard said, "I appreciate your earnestness. But no need for promises. I know you'll be back. You know this isn't so simple, and while I do hope you get your wife back soon, even with her in your arms, the Hull family is involved. They won't let this rest until they have all that they want."

Max nodded. "They don't want the painting either, do they?"

"It's just as much a map to them as it is to me."

"Okay, then. Get working on the painting. I'll get Sandra, and we'll be back to finish this thing."

Melinda returned with the printouts. Using a magnifying glass, Howard inspected the photos. "These are all good," he said and turned toward Max. "Take the painting. Get your

Sandra. But be very careful. This is the Hulls."

"I know. All too well."

# Chapter 16

When Max entered his office, he went straight for the bookcase and the whiskey. He would have to watch that or he'd be looking at an alcoholic in the mirror pretty soon.

With a startling clap of the hands, Drummond popped in. "That's the painting? You got it? Good work."

"I also got shot at."

As Max recounted his evening, the ghost detective smiled. "Just like my old days. This is great."

"Great? This is crap, and it's crap that's going to get Sandra killed. Now, come on. Stop being an ass and help me figure out the best way to exchange this thing for Sandra."

"For a start, you can calm down. You won't be any good if you go into this acting crazy." Max took another swig, put the flask back in the book, and slumped in his office chair. Floating in front of the painting, Drummond continued, "Now, you've done a good thing in getting Corkille to recreate this painting. That's an ace in our pocket. Of course, the big ace is the painting itself. So, once you're calm enough to think and speak clearly, you've got to call Connor and arrange a meeting."

"Where? When? You'll have to excuse me, but I've never dealt with a hostage negotiation before."

"Easy does it. I'll help you out."

Rage and tears filled out Max's chest. "I can't lose her. You understand that? She's everything to me."

All the amusement flushed from Drummond's pale face. In his kindest voice, he said, "Trust me, Max. We'll get her back."

Max looked at Sandra's empty desk, took a long breath, and eased back. "Okay," he whispered. "What do we do?"

"We need a location that's close enough so that I can be there. It should be public enough to protect you but secluded enough to not draw unwanted attention. And we need a time that's soon — before the world really starts waking up and getting on with the day. The longer we wait, the worse things have a chance of going. How long will Corkille take on the painting?"

"I've no idea. He's two hundred years old."

"But he's a spry two hundred."

In spite of himself, Max chuckled. Like popping a cork, laughter burst out of him until tears flowed from his eyes. Drummond said nothing. He just floated, waiting for Max to regain control, and Max appreciated it. They both knew this was the release he needed in order to keep functioning.

At length, Max dabbed at his eyes and said, "What about The Grand Theater?"

"The movie house?"

"It's a big eighteen screen theater with a huge parking lot. Nobody'll be there until the first shows — probably around noon. We could meet around the back for plenty of privacy but it's also public enough to satisfy — there are homes bordering one side and a major road with businesses on the other."

Drummond thought it over. "It's also just on the edge of the city. Plenty close for me to get around. Sounds perfect."

The phone call had been strange. Modesto had answered, not Connor. He ignored Max's questions and simply said that he would handle this negotiation. It surprised Max, not because he maintained a steady, in-control voice, but that Modesto didn't sound the least bit concerned. *He expected this all along.* Drummond warned that this whole thing might have been a set up — Modesto may have forced Connor into the kidnapping to make Max get the painting for them. But that much didn't matter to Max. He hated Modesto and Connor equally. Who cared which of them got the idea to use Sandra against him? They were both capable of it, and they both had plenty of sins to be punished for. Still, Modesto's behavior continued to strike Max oddly. Something wasn't quite right with that man.

* * *

The Grand Theater always looked like a warehouse club to Max. Large and boxy, the movie theater sat on the top of a high, flattened hill. Like a warehouse club, it mostly was a wide, paved parking lot. Around the side, near a green, dented dumpster, Max and Drummond waited in the car.

Dawn had just peeked over the trees, casting long shadows and orange light. Max sipped on hot, fast food coffee. Not very tasty but full of caffeine. Adrenaline had kept him going in short bouts, fear kept him up the rest of the night, but he felt sluggish after all these hours. He hoped the coffee would, at least, keep him alert until he had Sandra back.

"They're late," he said.

Drummond stared at the entrance to the lot. "They're fine. Don't get all cocked over a few minutes. A slow driver or a flat tire or any number of things can hold them up. Just keep remembering that they want this painting. If Connor is to be believed, they need this painting. So, they'll be here."

"I just wish it were over."

"Stay focused on the moment, and before you know it, it will be over. You remember what you've got to do?"

"What's to remember? Give the painting, get Sandra. It's a straight-forward exchange." Max turned on Drummond so fast, his hot coffee splashed a bit on his hand. Whipping his wet hand out the window, he sprayed the coffee onto the ground. "You're not planning on anything stupid, are you? They've got Sandra. Don't you screw this up."

Drummond rolled his dead eyes. "You have got to learn how this game is played. You really think they'll just walk up and make a fair exchange? That never happens. Never. Even if they do give you Sandra, they'll try something, some way to bring the leverage back onto them."

"Isn't that why Corkille's copying the painting?"

"That's not enough. Chances are they'd kill Corkille, Melinda, and you and Sandra if they found out about that.

Heck, they already killed the previous owner and they tried to kill you. This painting is extremely important to them."

"We don't know who shot at me for sure."

"Maybe you can ask them. They're here."

A car more beaten than Max's Honda clunked along the parking lot. Two men were visible inside as the car shuddered to a halt several feet away. Nobody moved for a bit as if the cars themselves were sizing each other up.

With an impatient sigh, Max reached behind, grabbed the painting, and stepped out of the car. Drummond slid through the car door and floated nearby. "Be careful," he said.

Max held back a sarcastic reply. He didn't need these henchmen to see him talking to thin air.

The two men stepped from their car. Max recognized the heavyset man right away — Mr. Gold, owner of the Deacon Art Gallery. With a shiver, Max also recognized the second man — a thin, blond man who was good with a sniper rifle and, apparently, at impersonations.

"Do you have a real name, Blondie, or should I call you Mr. Hull?" Max said. Blondie's lips lifted in a grin that lacked all sense of amusement.

Drummond swooped by them all and peered into the car. "She's in here. Tied up and laying low. She looks okay. Not hurt. Not frightened. Really, she looks more angry than anything else."

Max wanted to laugh. That was his Sandra all right.

"Let's keep this simple," Blondie said. "Mr. Gold will verify the painting, and assuming he gives it an okay, we'll release your wife."

"I don't see my wife," Max said. He had to play his part well, and he figured the further away from their car she was, the safer she would be.

Blondie glared at Max for a brief instant before turning back to the car. He opened the back door and yanked Sandra out. She looked exactly as Drummond had said — unharmed and angry.

"Hi, Sugar," Drummond said and Sandra's eyes flickered in

his direction as she tried to take in the situation.

"I believe this is yours," Blondie said, pushing her against the car hood. "Now, let Mr. Gold check out that painting."

"Of course," Max said. He placed the painting on the asphalt and took three steps back.

As Mr. Gold proceeded to examine the painting, Drummond whispered something in Sandra's ear before blocking her from view with his body. Max tried not to watch them too closely or else he'd draw Blondie's suspicions, but he was suspicious himself. Drummond winced in pain but continued whatever he was attempting.

"Well, well," Mr. Gold said, "Max here has been busy. He found the painting underneath *Mourning in Red.* The real painting. Shame you had to remove the top painting in such a brutal manner. I could have lifted it and saved both artworks."

"Neither is really that good," Max said.

"Art can have great value even when it's bad."

Blondie spit off to the side. "Enough with the college debate. Is it what we want or not?"

Flashing a distasteful sneer, Mr. Gold said, "It's what we want."

"Good, then all we need to do now is kill them both."

Drummond's head jutted up for just a second, then he furiously returned to Sandra. Max finally understood — Drummond was undoing her ropes. For a ghost to do such a thing — an act that required dexterity and patience, and an act that would cause a ghost a lot of pain — left Max awestruck.

He would have stared with his mouth agape had not Drummond snapped, "Max, stall him or we're all dead."

This woke him up. Max said, "You can't kill us. We have a copy of the Hull family journal. If we get harmed, that journal will go public. It'll take the family apart. And somehow, I don't think they'll look on you too kindly over that."

Blondie pulled a gun from his jacket pocket — a small, stubby looking thing that, Max had no doubt, could pop a hole right through his skull. "I'm not Hull, and I don't work for him. You want to destroy that family, go right ahead. It'll make life a lot easier on the rest of us."

"You work for Hull's witch. Same thing."

"Not to me."

"But the witch only wants this painting for Hull."

"Lots of people want this thing. If the stories are to be believed, this holds some serious mojo. Me, I don't care at all. I just want to get paid to do my job and I'll be on my way. And right now, my job is to make sure there are no loose ends."

"What about you, Mr. Gold?"

Drummond gave an enthusiastic nod. "That's right. Just keep them talking. Almost got this."

Max took several steps closer to Mr. Gold. "You really okay with murdering my wife and me?"

"I ... I ..."

"See that, Blondie? I don't think he's on board with your plans," Max said. He surprised himself with the firmness of his voice when he knew his insides were jittering as if electrocuted. "I think Mr. Gold is realizing that no matter who you work for that person isn't as powerful as the Hull family. I think he's wondering what kind of lunatic he signed on with."

With a flick of the wrist, Blondie turned the little gun onto Sandra. But Sandra wasn't there. She had stepped to the side and swung her newly-freed fist into his jaw. He lurched to the right and flailed out his hand, sending the little gun into the distance.

Max sprung toward Mr. Gold as Sandra pulled back for another strike on Blondie. The well-trained sniper, however, had other plans. He caught Sandra mid-swing with his forearm and shoved her back against the car.

Mr. Gold held the painting in front of him like a shield. Max felt a stab of pity. Had Corkille not been busily recreating the painting, Mr. Gold's shield would be worth something. As it was, Max had no problem punching through the canvas and into Mr. Gold's gut.

"No," Mr. Gold cried out, scrambling off toward the theater entrance with the damaged painting hooked on one arm, the other cradling his stomach.

Max turned back to see Sandra and Blondie grappling on the ground, rolling toward the little gun. "Drummond! A little help!"

Drummond had been standing near the gun, kicking it out of reach every time Blondie got close. He looked at Max and said, "What more do I have to do? She's putting up a good fight."

"Help her, damn it!"

Sandra wrenched Blondie over, straddled him, and threw a mean jab into his nose. His head snapped back and smacked hard on the pavement. Dazed by the blow, his eyes rolled without focus.

Sandra stood up and massaged her hand. "Get the gun, Max," she said. "And I'm going to need some ice."

Drummond shook his head and laughed. "One hell of a woman."

# Chapter 17

MAX DROVE SOUTH ALONG ROUTE 52. They stopped at a gas station for some ice to wrap around Sandra's hand before crossing over to Peters Creek Parkway and down to the Corkille house. Drummond hovered over the back, his arms stretched across the seat like a satisfied king.

"You both did an excellent job back there," he said. "Really top notch. Not only did we get Sandra back safely, but Max, my boy, you ruined that painting. Superb."

Max did not share Drummond's enthusiasm. "I'm just glad Sandra's okay."

"Don't worry about me," she said. "They didn't mistreat me or anything like that. The worst was when they took me. I didn't know what was happening and that was scary. But once they got me to this little apartment, they were very business-like. Dr. Connor came by once to make sure they didn't try anything stupid with me."

Drummond said, "Best to be vigilant right now. Connor's angry at us, and an angry witch is not something to underestimate."

"No risk of that," Sandra said. "She made it all too clear what she would do if Max didn't come through. Believe me, the curses she said she would cast were far worse than living forever or being a bound ghost."

"Hey, I am a bound ghost. It ain't no picnic."

"How about having your genitals dry up and wither away? Max'll be the recipient of that pleasant curse. And for me, she plans to make me barren."

Max couldn't hide the rising pitch in his voice. "W-What? Can she do those things for real?"

"I'm not sure just how powerful witches can actually

become. But I know this much — spells against a person require them to be at the casting. She can't do them remotely. So, we're okay, for now. Just don't get caught by her."

Thinking about the time she had tried to curse him before, Max shivered. "I really hate that woman."

Sandra reached out and Max took her hand. As the car sped down the road, their fingers entwined. Max brought her hand to his lips and kissed her fingers.

"I know things have been tough with us, but when I thought I might not get you back — it killed me."

Sandra laid her other hand on top of his, but her eyes remained focused on the road ahead. Max wished he had the right words to say that would let her know just how much he felt for her, but she was a smart woman — smart enough to know that people feel extra passionate after a life and death ordeal. Anything he said, anything he did at this moment would just be dismissed as the results of adrenaline and facing one's mortality.

But she had put her hand on his. She didn't pull away. And from other things she had said and done since this case began, Max gained a little hope. She still loved him. He knew that much. He only needed to break down those protective walls they had both constructed.

The rest of the drive proceeded in silence. Even Drummond had the sense to keep quiet. When they pulled into the Corkille's horseshoe drive, the morning sun was fully in the sky.

Melinda Corkille came out to meet them with a warm smile, but her bloodshot eyes and trembling hands spoke to the long night they had all endured. She watched Sandra get out of the car, and her warm smile fell away. Sandra caught the change, and the two women appraised each other without a word.

Before Max could say anything to diffuse them, Sandra looked at him and said, "Two hundred years old? She doesn't look a day over one-fifty."

"Ouch," Drummond said with an amused click of the tongue. "I think you're going to scorch her with your eyes, Sugar."

Max forced a chuckle. "Honey, let me introduce you to Melinda Corkille. Howard's the immortal one."

"That's right. I forgot."

Melinda refused to take the bait. "Come on, Max. Howard's been working all night. He's almost done."

As they entered the house, Max tried to ignore the frosty glower his wife sent his way. *Deep down,* he reminded himself, *she loves me.* This was just jealousy, and for nothing, because he had done nothing more than been tempted. If men were to be found guilty of infidelity for simply being tempted, there wouldn't be a faithful man alive.

"Melinda!" Howard's voice cracked as he yelled for her.

"Come on," Melinda said with an exasperated huff. "I'm glad I wasn't around when he was in his prime. The man has been insufferable since he got to work on the painting."

They followed Melinda into Howard's studio. The photographs they had taken earlier were pinned on cork boards surrounding the canvas. Most of the painting had been completed and Max had to admire the man's work.

It looked exactly as he recalled the original looked. Not just the obvious details — the dark figure in the doorway, the strong brush strokes, the eerie quality of the painting's mood — but also the smaller details — the thickness of the paint in certain areas, so thick it formed a hill on the canvas; the delicate blending of color; the distressed chipping of poorly made paints dried and abused over years. All of it had been recaptured by Howard Corkille's talented hands.

"Remarkable work," Max said.

Howard beamed. "If for nothing else, I want to thank you for giving me an excuse to break out my paints again. It's felt wonderful to be in front of the canvas once more."

Melinda hugged Howard's shoulders and kissed the top of his head. "Have you found what we need?"

"Sit," Howard said, waving everybody to find a stool or chair. Even Drummond settled on a worktable. Max caught Sandra's eye and grinned. Sandra kept a stoic face.

"I swear, the two of you are hopeless," Drummond said.

Before Sandra or Max could react, Howard cleared his throat and spoke. "You all know that magic is real. One look at me will tell you that much. What you may not know is that magic is quite active and quite common. Those who practice at it use spells and curses all the time. It happened more long ago because more people understood about these kinds of things. One of those people was a man named Edward Teach. Do you know that name?"

"It sounds familiar," Max said. He could picture a page in a history text but nothing more.

"He was born in England sometime around 1680. He became fond of the sea and worked for a while as a seaman in Jamaica. Most of this man's life is shadowed in unconfirmed reports, and his surname of Teach isn't even accurate. It's just a name historians chose to give him because men in his line of work often went by numerous fictitious names. They had to call him something and I suppose they had some source that named him such, so they went with it."

"What line of work was he in?" Sandra asked.

Howard rocked his hands on his knees. "He was a pirate. A very successful one. Took the French ship *Concord* as a prize and converted her into a pirate ship of his own design. He called her *Queen Anne's Revenge,* and his name was —"

"Blackbeard," Max said, his eyes wide. He examined the dark figure in the painting again. "That's Blackbeard?"

"Yes. Sort of. See back when Blackbeard was Edward Teach, his success had been more of the failure kind. At one point, it is thought he considered giving the whole notion up. But on a drunken night in Jamaica, he met with a voodoo priestess, and he struck a deal. Nobody knows, of course, what exactly happened, but Blackbeard was born that night — that much is certain.

"He had always been a big man, but when he left Jamaica, he had become huge. And he had built an image with a great, black beard that he braided into pigtails and tied off with colorful ribbons. He strapped numerous weapons to his clothing, and, most notoriously, he weaved cannon cord into his hair so that he could light it and appear that much more menacing to his adversaries.

"But it was more than that." The group listened to Howard like captivated children around a teacher. "The lighting of his hair was part of the magic spell that had been conjured for him. Without it, he would've just been Edward Teach. Now, two things happened to him that matter to us. The first is that in 1718, King George I sent Captain Rogers to govern New Providence, where Blackbeard had been based. Rogers was the kind of man who would cause Blackbeard trouble, so Blackbeard picked up and moved his entire operation to North Carolina. It's a perfect location — close to the Gulf Stream, excellent places to exploit like Cape Fear, and a ready market in Bath Town for his gains. Not only that but he sold directly at the market and cut out the middle men.

"The second thing of importance to us is that Blackbeard had a soft spot for women. Even fell in love and married quite a few. Several at the same time. But the one true love in his life was the one woman who had any real power over him."

"The voodoo priestess," Max said.

"Exactly. The legend is that when she learned of all his infidelity to her, she traveled to North Carolina and took him to bed. When he awoke, she was gone — and so was his famed burning hair. Not long after this, his career as a pirate and his life came to an end."

Sandra gestured to the painting. "So, this is Blackbeard in the doorway watching while his priestess performs a spell on the floor?"

"Sort of," Howard said. "I'll get to the painting in a moment, but it doesn't come into the story just yet."

"Have a little patience," Melinda said. Sandra ignored her.

"Now," Howard went on, "what we are interested in here is those strands of Blackbeard's hair, the ones imbued with magic. You see, there's only one way to really keep a secret. Do you know it?"

Max nodded. "Don't tell anyone."

"Old Blackbeard never was good at secrets. Many people

knew of his magic burning hair, and after the priestess reclaimed it, many of these unsavory types sought her out. Because this kind of magic doesn't die until the object is destroyed."

"Like a binding curse," Drummond said.

"Afraid for her life, and rightfully so, the priestess hid the hairs with the thought that she would reclaim its magic once the world stopped trying to find her. She had many lovers and one of them, a young artist living on the beaches, became the recipient of a beautiful new paintbrush with the finest bristles made of the strangest hairs."

"You're joking," Max said. "That's what this is about? A paintbrush?"

"That paintbrush has fallen into many different hands and crossed many oceans over the years, but it always manages to get back here. Twice in my life, I've had the opportunity to get hold of it and use its magic to break my curse. Twice it slipped away."

"This painting here, this one depicting the spell's creation, you think it can show us where the brush is?"

"I know it can."

"Then stop telling us stories and show us where."

"I'm well aware of your urgency. I think mine is greater. But without knowing the full background, you'd waste more time with tons of questions that would just have made me tell it all anyway. And so, I have one more thing to explain, and that is this painting."

All eyes took in the painting once more. Knowing what the painting actually depicted did little to ease Max's tensions over the entire case. With only a year under his belt since extricating himself from the horrible situation with the Hull family, he hated the idea that he was tied up with them once more. But this time it appeared that all roads led to them. Even a road that began with Blackbeard the pirate. Just thinking that churned Max's stomach.

And yet — he had to admit that he kind of liked the whole experience. A little. He didn't like being shot at, nobody would like that, but at the same time, he got a sense of why some soldiers can't leave the wars they fight. More than just an adrenaline rush, being shot at, being caught in a dangerous situation, being the target of a powerful family — it all filled Max with a sense of life. As if his heart could only beat under the pressure of these horrible tensions.

He glanced at Drummond and saw it on the old ghost's face. That's why Drummond stuck around. With the binding curse broken, Drummond could easily move on to wherever he truly belonged, but he didn't want to go. He wanted that same high that Max felt. And the fact that a ghost could feel it too proved that it wasn't just adrenaline. After all, a ghost doesn't have adrenaline.

Howard pointed out several brush strokes on the canvas, cleared his throat, and said, "This painting of Blackbeard's cursed deal is unique for many reasons. First off, there are no real pictures of the man. We don't know what he looked like. He loved for his women to be the subject of a portrait but always managed to stay off the painter's canvas."

"Is that why he's a shadowy figure here? The artist had no idea what he looked like," Sandra said.

"Yes. But these brush strokes tell me a lot more. Earlier I told Max that this painting was a map. Well, the brush strokes are the key. They tell me that the artist who created this was a man named Jules Korner and he lived about thirty minutes north of here in Kernersville. I know these strokes so well because I'm the one who taught Jules how to do it."

# Chapter 18

MAX HAD TO WILL HIS FOOT to ease off the gas. He didn't want to be pulled over and given a ticket just because his body felt the urgency to get to the Korner home as fast as possible. Sandra sat next to him and placed one hand on his shoulder.

Howard had given them the basic idea. In the 1870s, Jules Korner ran an interior decorating business to augment his painting career. He became most famous for two things — first, he painted the Bull Durham bulls all across the South. These bulls, the symbol for Durham tobacco, were painted on barns and walls all over. Each time, Korner made them anatomically correct, if not exaggerated. He then contacted local papers and, posing as a concerned citizen, complained about the lewd image. Soon enough, everyone knew the Durham bull.

Korner's second claim was his home, dubbed "Korner's Folly." Completed in 1880, the house served both as a showcase and a home. No two doors, no two fireplaces (there were fifteen), no two rooms, were alike. Also, the entire attic had been converted into America's first private little theater. As Max took the on-ramp to Business 40 East, he wondered if the home could live up to its title as "The Strangest House in the World" or if this was just another one of Korner's publicity stunts.

Before they had left, Howard said, "Jules was an eccentric man but he was smart. He was crazy enough to paint this and yet smart enough to cover it up. You'll see when you go to his house. I'm sure that somewhere in there is either that paintbrush or a clue to finding it."

Max didn't know how much faith to put into Howard's idea, but he saw few options at the moment. He did have the sense to send Drummond out searching for Jules Korner's ghost. Perhaps the man would be willing to help.

"It's coming up," Sandra said, pointing to Exit 14 for Kernersville.

Melinda had opted to stay with Howard, and Max felt grateful he didn't have to find some excuse to leave her behind. Though he had managed to avoid Melinda's advances, he knew Sandra sensed something wrong, and a surge of guilt had struck him. It wasn't enough to just be faithful. He had to make sure Sandra knew in her heart how much he loved her.

"When this is over," he said, "you and I are taking a vacation."

Sandra nodded. "We can't afford one, but the thought is nice."

They couldn't miss the house. Its rust-colored, pointy roof cut high into the air. Numerous chimneys poked up from the structure, while the stone- and brick-work drew the eye down to the enormous body of the house. A wide field off to the side with a gravel drive served as the parking area.

"It looks like a haunted house from an old black-and-white fright movie," Max said. "I love it."

They paid for tickets and walked to the front of the house. The porch wrapped around, mostly lined in beautiful brick designs, and the flooring had been done with little mosaic tiles. Near the entrance, Sandra pointed to a small, cauldron-shaped pot nestled underneath a brick shelving. In front of the pot, the tiling read WITCHES CORNER — though the T had been chipped off.

"Not what you're thinking," Max said. "A 'Witches Corner' is an old European tradition. Whenever you were going in or out of the house, you were supposed to put coins in the pot so that any evil spirits nearby would be distracted. That way you could enter or exit in peace. It's not real. Not like Dr. Connor."

"You sure about that?"

Max took a long look at the rusting pot. Then he dug out a quarter and tossed it in. Sandra patted his arm as they walked inside.

The foyer was a small, cluttered space with four doors, all different heights, shapes, and styles. Through a small opening off to the right, Max saw a narrow staircase — connecting to nothing, as far as he could tell. Korner's self-portrait hung to the side of one doorway — an eerie-looking man in a dark suit with the strangest expression on his face as if he could see all these people coming in and counted them all as fools. The ceiling had a painting of two cherubs. It was like walking into the Mad Hatter's home as designed by M. C. Escher.

"Welcome to Korner's Folly," a middle-aged woman said. "May I have your tickets, please?"

As the lady collected the tickets and launched into her introduction speech, Max glanced through the glass on the doorway behind her. He saw a long room with huge, black furniture and a ceiling taller than in the foyer — and on that ceiling, he saw a painting.

"Excuse me," he said and ignored the flustered scowl of the lady. "Are there paintings on every ceiling?"

"Not all. But most. The ceilings are quite interesting, actually. Some of the ceilings are as high as twenty-five feet, and some, like in the children's rooms, are just under six feet. This space was originally used for horses and —"

"And did Jules Korner paint all of them himself?"

The lady forced a smile. "No. He designed them all, but another man painted them. In fact, he designed all the furnishings in this house, and he —"

"I thought Korner was a painter."

"He was," she said, her words clipped. "Most of the paintings you'll find on the walls throughout the house are by Jules Korner. Now, if you'll let me finish, I'll be glad to take any further questions after I'm done."

Max pantomimed zipping up his lips and let the lady complete her job. He tried to listen closely, but his eyes kept trying to snatch a peek of the house beyond. When she finished, she turned her eyes to Max and asked if there were any questions.

With a shake of his head, Max said nothing. Sandra,

however, spoke up. "Did you just say this house is haunted?"

Max had not been listening closely and had missed this part. Now he focused intently on the answer. The lady offered an embarrassed smile. "A few years ago, the North Carolina Paranormal Society conducted several tests over a few nights and, according to them, this house is officially haunted. Now, I've been working here for almost ten years, and I've never heard or seen anything."

"Is it supposed to be Jules Korner?"

"I don't know about that. To the best of my knowledge, nothing tragic ever happened here and certainly not to Jules Korner. Don't make a deal out of it. It's just silliness. Now, if there are no further questions ..."

She opened the glass-paned door and ushered them into the rest of the house. The tour was self-guided from that point on. Numbered placards could be found in each room describing the history of the room and noting features. At the bottom of the placard were instructions on where to go next.

Max and Sandra walked through the house like any other touring couple except for where their eyes went. Sandra appeared to be most interested in the dark, open, empty spaces of the house. Max watched her closely at the entrance of each room, hoping to see on her face if she discovered a ghost. Then his eyes examined every painting and mural he could find.

He looked closely for brush strokes similar to the ones in "Mourning in Red." He didn't expect to find some secret clue. Rather he wanted to find proof that Howard Corkille had told them the truth. That this trip to Korner's Folly wasn't really Corkille's folly.

About halfway through the house they climbed an open staircase and entered the children's rooms. Max had to duck because everything in the room, including the ceiling, had been designed for a child's height. It was like being in a giant dollhouse, and despite the ample daylight, Max's skin prickled.

He looked to Sandra. "Anything?" he asked.

Her face had paled and she nodded. "I'm not so sure who it is, though. I can only see a blurry image."

Max frowned. "Has that ever happened before?"

"Not often. It's usually somebody who is both here and there."

"There?"

"The afterlife that most ghosts can't find or are trying to avoid. But sometimes they get stuck. They start to move on and then maybe they can't fully let go or they lose their way or something. Whatever the case, they end up a little bit in both worlds and that makes them blurry."

"Can you talk to them? Can they hear you?"

"I can try," she said but the sounds of footsteps climbing the stairs ushered them on to the next room. A family of five was right behind them showing their impatience as if they were waiting for a turn at mini-golf and Max was holding up the line.

Later, Max and Sandra entered the reception room, a large ball room on the second floor — or maybe it was the third or fourth floor, the house had so many stairs and ups and downs it became difficult to know for sure. In a glass booth, Max saw the most frightening marionettes — one a copy of each member of the family. They had exaggerated features and old, chipped paint.

"Sandra."

When she walked over and saw the marionette family, she let out a gasp. "I'd rather see ghosts," she said.

"They would be a good place to hide a magic brush."

When they reached the attic, Sandra grasped Max's hand with crushing strength. The entire floor had been converted into a theater with a wooden thrust stage at one end and chairs all around. Off to the right was a large replica of the house with the center cut out and curtained — a puppet theater. The ceiling raised up to a point and on their slanted sides were eight enormous murals.

But Max knew that the impressive sight had not caused Sandra's reaction. "How many do you see?" he whispered.

"I don't know. They're all blurring together." Sandra's skin turned bone white, and she leaned in to Max's shoulder. "I don't feel so good."

Without another word, Max escorted her through the house, not worrying about the proper tour path, and garnering a few perturbed glares from other visitors. He led Sandra outside, and the fresh air had an immediate effect on her. Her skin regained some color as she took long, deep breaths.

"You okay?" Max asked.

Sandra nodded. "I don't know what happened. It was just so strange. In my whole life, I've seen maybe three of those blurry ghosts. But up there ... I can't believe how many there were."

"Does that mean the paintbrush ..." Max's voice trailed off as his eyes looked toward the parking lot. He could feel Sandra's quizzical stare falter and felt her shift as she followed his gaze. He heard her breath catch.

Dr. Connor and Mr. Modesto leaned against the old Honda.

# Chapter 19

"DID YOU ENJOY YOUR TOUR?" Dr. Connor asked. She looked much healthier than at any other time in the past few days. She also looked like somebody savoring her own maliciousness.

"Get off my car," Max said.

Mr. Modesto gazed down to indicate that he did not actually touch the car. The sneer on his face showed that he wouldn't touch the car even if given permission. Dr. Connor, on the other hand, pressed harder against the car door.

"Mr. Porter, let me begin by assuring you that you will not find the object which you are seeking," Mr. Modesto said. He spoke a bit slower than normal, choosing each word with great care and purpose. "However tarnished by you, we still possess the actual painting. We have all the information required and we have a greater desire to acquire this object. So, if you will simply let this go, we can get this object for our employer and no further contact between us will be necessary. Your insurance policy that you so gleefully hold over us will continue to be honored, of course."

"Get off that car, now," Sandra said. Even from his peripheral vision, Max could see that Sandra was about to take a swing at Connor. Perhaps the witch sensed it, too, because she did take one step away — smiling the whole time.

"Furthermore," Mr. Modesto said and threw a distasteful look at Connor, "I believe this woman owes you an apology."

Connor locked eyes with Mr. Modesto just long enough to show that she hated doing this, that he had forced her, and that she didn't mean a single word. She faced Max and Sandra with her mocking grin. "I'm sorry for taking you from your husband, and I'm sorry for causing you so much trouble. The Hull family had no part in it."

"Thank you," Mr. Modesto said. Dr. Connor threw in a patronizing curtsy and stepped back.

Max leaned in towards Mr. Modesto. "Y'know, you keep coming to me with apologies. First, Mr. Gold and now Dr. Connor. The Hull family should look closer at their hiring practices."

"Undoubtedly. They hired you, after all."

Max let out a slight laugh. "And, thankfully, I don't work for them anymore. So, I don't take their orders, either. It's been nice chatting with you. Now, if you'll please move aside, we have to confer with our client."

"Am I to take that to mean you're still going to pursue these matters?"

"Take it any way you want."

"You won't find it. We have the painting. And we know exactly where the object is."

Sandra pushed Connor aside as she stormed to the car door. "It's called a paintbrush. We all know it, so stop with all the 'this object' nonsense. And the answer is no. We are not backing out of this case. Besides, you're a bad liar. You have no clue where this paintbrush is."

Connor came up to the car door and shoved it closed just as Sandra got in, narrowly missing her fingers. "We know exactly where it is. We just have to wait for the right time to get it."

"Dr. Connor," Modesto snapped.

The witch backed away from the car, pulled out a hip flask, and swung back its contents. "I'm watching you," she said and waved a finger at Sandra — naughty, naughty.

As Max started the car, Sandra raised a finger of her own.

They drove straight to the office without a word. Sandra fumed while Max tried to replay the entire conversation in his head. Something didn't sit right. Something felt off in the way Modesto spoke.

When they entered the office, Max felt a surprising twinge of disappointment that Drummond was not to be found. He settled behind his desk, propped up his feet, and got lost in thought. Sandra tapped away at her computer.

"They close at four o'clock," she said.

"Who?"

"Korner's Folly. The house closes at four. I'm assuming you want to go there tonight to see what we can find."

"What about the blurry ghosts?"

Sandra shrugged. "Guess I won't be going into the theater."

"Honey, I don't know if —"

"Don't even start. You know we have to go. Besides, that bitch-witch said they knew where the paintbrush was, they just had to wait for the right time. It's got to be in that house. They wouldn't have come all that way just to mouth off at us."

"No, but if Hull told them to do so, they certainly would come to make sure we had accepted that apology. They don't want those journals released."

"Maybe. But they had to be scoping out the house, too. And it seems they think they know where it is."

Max nodded. "Which means they'll be going after it tonight."

"That's why we have to get there first."

Scratching his chin, Max pictured the house. "We'll all have to wait until dark. Even then, the house is right on a major street. I don't see how we're going to get in without attracting unwanted attention. Not to mention we've got to get in, find the paintbrush, and get out before Hull's people show up. You got any bright ideas?"

Before Sandra could answer, Drummond burst in the office from the bookcase. "I've got an idea," he said as he swooped into a chair.

Startled, Max sat forward, banging his knee on the desk. "I can't believe you. Have you been here the whole time? Just eavesdropping from your bookcase?"

Drummond dismissed the accusation with a shrug. "Seemed like a smart thing to do at the time."

"Don't you trust us?"

"More than most people, but until you're a ghost floating

around this office with me, I've got to protect myself now and then. Oh, get over yourself — I wasn't eavesdropping. I only caught the end of what you were saying. Okay, Mr. Uppity-uppity?"

Max crossed his arms and rolled his eyes. "Fine. I've got more important things to worry about. Like have you found Jules Korner yet?"

Drummond leaned back and glanced at Sandra. "He thinks I wouldn't have told him about that already? C'mon."

"Then why are you here and not looking for him?"

"Because sometimes you have to be calm, put out your feelers, and wait. I've spread the word in the right ears, and I need to wait a little to see if Korner shows up. Now, do you want to hear my idea, or do you want to sulk around your office for a few hours?"

Sometimes Max wished Drummond had a more substantial body, so he could smack the ghost hard. "Tell us your idea," he said, slouching back in his chair.

Bringing his hands together with one, sharp clap, Drummond popped into the air and looked at both his partners. "I could go to the house right now. Nobody can see me, so I can search for this paintbrush while the tours are still going on. Then, when evening comes, you guys show up, and I guide you to where it is — or at least, where it isn't, if I haven't found it by then."

Max let Drummond hang in the air with an expectant gaze. He knew the idea was good. It didn't take a genius to see that. But he still felt ruffled by Drummond and wanted the ghost to stew a bit.

Sandra misinterpreted Max's hesitation for doubt, and said, "That's one of the best ideas I've ever heard from you. Go do it, and we'll meet you at Korner's Folly tonight. It's not too far, is it? I mean, you won't get snapped back like you did on our way to Lake Norman?"

"I don't think so," Drummond said, but he didn't seem so confident. "I suspect it's close to the edge of my territory, though, so I might be in a bit of pain. You might have to nurse me a bit when I get back."

Sandra shook her head. "Just get going."

"Sugar, you're a heartbreaker."

Sandra laughed as Drummond flew out of the office. When she turned around, Max had not moved from his desk. His old anger had ignited deep in his gut, and he could see on his wife's face that she knew it, too.

"I don't want to fight," she said, picking at some papers on her desk.

"This is so messed up. You're flirting with a dead guy right in front of me while I'm feeling guilty over Melinda Corkille when nothing happened."

Sandra slammed the papers down. "I knew something was going on with that woman."

"Nothing went on. I mean, she tried, but I wasn't buying."

"But you feel guilty."

"I'm a man. I have thoughts even if I'm strong enough not to act on them. And frankly, things haven't been all that wonderful between us lately, so you shouldn't be surprised that I'm having thoughts."

"Really?" Sandra said in a tone that spewed fire and brimstone. "Is that the way it is for men? The second we have a little marital spat, you just start thinking about screwing other women?"

Max was on his feet now. "Honey, guys think about screwing other women all the time. It has nothing to do with our marriage or love or anything. It's just the way we're wired."

"So what's your problem then? It's okay for you to flirt with Melinda but if I sass Drummond just for fun it's wrong? What kind of fucked up logic goes on in your brain?"

"I'm not mad about that," Max shouted. "I'm not angry at all!"

His thundering voice echoed in the building. Sandra locked eyes with him, both of them seething, and before another word could be yelled, she processed his words and the corner of her mouth trembled upward. The other corner also moved up until she fully smiled.

"This is serious," Max said, but the end of his words were caught in a laugh.

"I know," she said, and stepped back, covering her mouth.

That did it. The two of them burst into hysterics. Sandra collapsed at her desk, clutching her stomach, and letting out laughter with abandon. Max's eyes watered as he followed suit.

So much of their stress poured out with each successive wave that once their bodies got started, stopping seemed impossible. Max's sides ached yet every time they thought it ended, a snort or chuckle would send them off again. And if felt good. More than just a release, the moment brought with it relief.

At length, they managed to speak with only a few giggles breaking through. Max dabbed at his eyes and said, "I swear, honey, you have nothing to worry about. I love you. I always have."

"Then trust me. And I don't mean about jealousy. I know you trust me there, and I know you don't really think anything about Drummond. But in the rest of our life, you've got to trust me."

"I do."

"No, you don't." She stepped near Max and wrapped her arms around his waist. "How long have you been sitting here in this office wishing I'd leave? Hmmm? It's driving you nuts having me here. You said it the other day that you feel smothered. But you're stuck because business is bad and I'm an asset you can't do without right now. I get it. It's tough. But you think it's a picnic being around you all day?"

Max smiled. "Maybe not a picnic, but surely a nice snack."

"Don't flatter yourself." She playfully slapped his chest. "Look, unless you gain the ability to see all the ghosts like I have, you're stuck with me."

"I don't mind having you here."

"Yes, you do. But that's okay. Couples aren't meant to be glued together all the time. We'd kill each other while professing how much we love one another."

"Then what do we do?"

"I don't know." They both let out a short laugh. "But now that we're actually talking again, I do know that we can figure it out. We make a pretty smart team."

Max hugged his wife tight and strong. "You're an incredible woman. Far more than I ever deserved."

"Don't forget it," she said and wiped her eyes on his shoulder. "Now, let's go find that stupid paintbrush."

# Chapter 20

MAX AND SANDRA HAD TO KILL a few hours before it would be safe to go out to Korner's Folly. They drove to T.J.s Deli, scarfed a few sandwiches — eating too fast from nerves — and they waited. As worrisome as the whole situation had become, a small part of Max enjoyed sitting with Sandra at the deli. It was such a simple, normal thing to do. So unlike their everyday lives that he had to stop just long enough to etch the moment into his brain.

And then it was time to go.

They drove in silence but not a quiet boiling with anger. Nerves, of course, but the tension between them had disappeared. Now, Max could focus entirely on the job at hand.

"I want you to be my getaway man," Max said as they neared the off ramp for Kernersville. "This house is so visible. I need you to stay in the car, keep it running, honk if you see a cop or Modesto or anybody really. If I come running out, open the passenger door and be ready to get us out of there. You okay with that?"

"I can be a getaway gal, if that works for you."

Max smiled. "My apologies. 'Getaway gal' sounds much better."

They pulled in the visitor parking lot and drove onto the grass behind the house. It wasn't completely out of sight, but anybody passing in a car would probably miss them. If someone came by on foot, however, they were in trouble.

Max kissed Sandra on the cheek and headed toward the building. He moved to the side entrance (which was used as the exit from the tour) and tried the doorknob. Locked.

"Drummond," Max hissed as loud as he dared. "Drummond."

No answer. He slid along the wall toward the front of the house, trying to stay behind the various brick walls. From the corner, he saw no easy way to get to the front door. It was probably locked anyway. As he started to turn back, he glimpsed the beaten pot in front of the words WITCHES CORNER.

*Why not?* He dug out a dime and a nickel and tossed them into the pot. The dull clink seemed loud to his ears, but nobody appeared to notice.

"Drummond," he whispered again as he hurried back to the side door. "Come on. Open up."

The side door lock clicked. Max stared at it as if he had never seen one before. Then he tried the knob and found it opened with ease. He stepped into a long room — the sewing room, if he recalled correctly from the tour — it was hard to tell in the dark. He had a small penlight with him but didn't want to use it unless he had no other choice. With so many windows in the house, he feared somebody might notice the light.

Drummond's ghostly visage seemed to shine pale light all around but didn't illuminate anything. It was a strange sight, one that Max had never noticed before. Drummond looked tired, even for a ghost.

"There's no paintbrush here. I've checked all but one room."

"What? Why didn't you just come back to the office and tell us not to bother?"

"Because it has to be in that room. I just can't go there."

"Out of your range?"

"No," Drummond said, glancing upward with a shiver. "It's not that. The room is at the very top — the attic that's a theater. But it's filled with the ghosts Sandra calls blurs. I can't go in there."

"Why not?"

"It hurts." Drummond turned away and let out an eerie sigh. Max thought, not for the first time, that Drummond could haunt a house to great effect. "I'm going back to the ghost realm. I'll find Jules Korner. He should be looking hard for me now, so it should be easy."

"Okay. I'll check out this theater. Don't worry about it."

"Who's worried?" Drummond said but he looked as if a giant arrow pointed at him.

Once his ghostly partner disappeared, Max headed deeper into the house. He flashed his penlight from time to time but never kept it on for more than a few seconds. The creaking wood floors and odd echoes made him think of a classic haunted house.

Every painting with a face followed his movements. He could feel their eyes upon him. From every ceiling mural, they looked down upon him. From every dark corner, every misshapen doorway, every narrow staircase, Max could feel the growing pressure of being watched.

Maybe he should have had Sandra come with him. The tour lady had said this place was officially haunted. Sandra would be able to see the ghosts, maybe even get them to talk.

As enticing as the idea of getting his wife by his side was, he knew he couldn't go back to get her. If he left this house, he wouldn't want to re-enter. Though not a believer of New Age-type things, he did believe that this place gave off a bad vibe. Something was wrong with this house. At least it felt that way at night, alone and in the dark.

After one wrong turn, he found the main stairwell that led up to the theater. He paused just long enough to feel his legs quiver and taste the dry coating in his mouth. Surely, Drummond could find out from Jules Korner where the paintbrush was hidden. Max didn't need to do this. Except there was no guarantee Drummond would find Korner let alone that the man would talk. And if Mr. Modesto was to be believed, time was not on Max's side. Through force of will, he moved upward, ignoring the strong desire to race back to Sandra, drive off, and never return.

When he reached the top, he found a lone figure standing on the stage — Blondie. The man wore a stylish suit like a true player of the nightclub scene, but his expression was one of impatience and malice. The hot attic air smelled of old wood like an ancient casket which gave Blondie a decidedly murderous aura.

"You sure took long enough," Blondie said. "Frankly, I don't understand why any of these people are worried about you. You can't seem to get any of this right. Although you sure screw things up a lot. No doubt about that."

"For you, I try my best," Max said, pleased that his voice wasn't shaking like his insides.

"Dr. Connor warned me about you. She said you had a smart mouth and a keen talent to get in the way. I figured she was just a little skittish because of your history with her. But it turns out she was right. I've got to know, though, before I kill you — why are you doing this? I mean, what do you gain by messing up things for Dr. Connor and Mr. Modesto? I don't get it."

Max thought about running, the words *before I kill you* often had that effect on him, but instead, he approached the edge of the stage, hoping to keep Blondie talking. He moved on instinct, something he continually tried to listen to more and more. And if his instincts weren't screaming for him to run, his brain must have heard something more important. And then it hit him. "*Messing up things for Dr. Conner and Mr. Modesto?* How?"

"I don't like it when people play coy or dumb, so stop it."

Max squinted in real confusion. "I don't understand. I saw them today. They've got the painting, you know that, they said they were going to beat me to the paintbrush. So, what exactly am I messing up, now?"

Blondie paced on the stage. "You really think this is just about getting some stupid brush? My, my, you are dumb. This, my stupid friend, this is about regaining their lives. Look at what you did to them. You ruined Dr. Connor's reputation and Hull pretty much cut her off from his family."

"Can't say I'm sorry. I don't really care about her. She tried to kill me once and she kidnapped my wife just recently. Seems to me, you were a part of that, too."

"Mr. Modesto didn't try to kill you. In fact, if anything, he's tried to help you navigate all these treacherous waters."

"I don't see it that way."

"Of course not. It's all about you, isn't it? What do you think happened to Mr. Modesto after you got hold of Hull's journal and held copies of it hostage?"

"That's my life insurance."

"I don't care what you call it. It pretty much ruined Mr. Modesto's standing, too. He's lucky they didn't kill him."

Max thought back to the strange dinner on Lake Norman, the one where Blondie pretended to be Terrance Hull. Mr. Modesto had handed Max the invitation. He knew Hull's schedule. He knew when the Lake Norman house would be clear. And that's why there were no servants, no chef, nobody around. That's why they tried to hire him to find the painting. Dr. Connor, Mr. Modesto, even Mr. Gold — they all were trying to get back into the embrace of the Hull family. And that thought brought with it another for the ride.

"Oh, I see," Max said, staring directly into Blondie's eyes. "It's not me that keeps screwing things up, it's you."

"Shut up."

"You failed to impersonate Hull well enough to get me to work for you. You failed to find the painting on your own and had to resort to kidnapping. And now, after all this, you've even failed to find the paintbrush. You just keep failing, don't you?"

Blondie's fingers curled into fists. Max's eyes darted around the room. He didn't see anybody else. Blondie said, "I suppose you found the paintbrush, then. Isn't that what you do? Find stuff nobody else can find?"

"You're pathetic. Not only did you fail at everything, but now you're standing here waiting for me to show up with the paintbrush so you can swipe it from me. No wonder Hull doesn't want to work with any of you. You can't do anything for yourselves."

"You watch that mouth of yours. It's going to get you in trouble."

"Wouldn't be the first time." Max looked over Blondie's

waist — no sign of a gun. That was odd. Every time before Blondie had a gun.

Following his eyes, Blondie said, "Not in here. Gunfire would get too much attention, and this place is full of so many little nooks, I might not be able to collect all my bullets should I miss my target. Don't want to leave anything behind for the cops."

"You didn't care about that out at the rest stop."

"Different location, different circumstances."

"Guess we can just add that to your list of failures."

Max had hoped to goad Blondie into making a mistake or revealing something important. He missed just how angry Blondie had become and was taken by surprise when the attack came.

"Bastard!" Blondie said and leaped off the stage. With his arms spread like a professional wrestler hulking in, he slammed onto Max, crashing them both to the floor. The big room echoed their grunts. Momentum took over, sliding them back and spinning them to the side.

Max felt his body roll and helped it along. He popped up on top of Blondie and punched the man's jaw. Blondie's head snapped back. But before Max could pull his fist back for another, Blondie struck hard into Max's sides, thudding against his kidneys.

As Max toppled over, Blondie got to his feet and kicked hard. Max rolled onto his back, every attempt to breathe bringing with it fiery pain below his ribcage. Moving with patience and power, Blondie straddled Max and gripped his throat with both hands.

"Where's the paintbrush?" Blondie said, barely moving his mouth.

"I don't have it," Max said, his voice betraying his fear.

Blondie tightened his grip. "Where is it?" he screamed, his face red, spit flying from his lips.

*He's lost his mind,* Max thought. He knew that kind of rage, and he knew that Blondie no longer was thinking about the paintbrush or Dr. Connor or Hull. He just wanted to release all his anger and Max was the object in his hands.

"Where is it?" Blondie screamed again and thumped Max's head against the floor.

Max tried to kidney punch Blondie, but he couldn't find the strength. His lungs strained for air. Little pale spots blinked into Max's vision.

He barely saw Blondie, now. His throat ached but even that pain started to lift. He had never asked Drummond what actual death was like, and now he wouldn't have to.

A flicker of a thought hit him. *Death.* He was dying. Those pale spots weren't from lack of air. He was dying — he could see the blurs, the ghosts! They drifted high above as if he were in the bottom of a giant fishbowl and they were the fish.

As Blondie cried out and clenched his throat, Max's eyes shot to the left. A little girl sat on the edge of the stage and watched. She wore a dress straight from the 19th century, and her cold, pale skin seemed to glow against the dress. The blurs hovered around her as she swung her feet. She cocked her head in interest.

Max reached out for her, pleading with his hands, his fingers, his eyes, everything he could — *Please, help me.* Tears dribbled from his eyes. *Please.* Even his lips trembled in an attempt to speak. *Help me.*

The little girl scooted back on the stage, her face startled. She clearly had not expected to be seen by the living. She stood and stared even longer at Max's face.

Watching this dead girl try to decide what to do seemed to last an eternity. He could hear a dim echo of Blondie's voice demanding to know the location of the paintbrush, but it was slow and distant. All he had rested on this ghost, and his mind could not think long on anything else.

As if seeing the full picture for the first time, the girl stepped closer. "Do you not want to die?" she asked.

Max wanted to snap a sarcastic, "What the hell do you think?" but it occurred to him that perhaps not all dead people thought in the same way as Drummond or as the living. Besides, it seemed best to just answer the question. He managed a tiny nod.

"Okay," the girl said.

She glanced upward at the blurs and spoke, but Max could not make out her words. The blurs understood, though. They all stopped their lazy drifting and stretched a bit in the girl's direction.

When the girl looked back at Max, the blurs swooped down, darting straight for Blondie. The first to arrive soared right through him. Blondie jerked to the side as if somebody had dropped an ice cube down his shirt.

Another blur passed through the other side, and Blondie jerked again. He looked around, confused. Then Max saw the change on the man's face — confusion turned to fear. The blurs sensed the change like sharks sensing blood. They shot in on Blondie's head, pushing together and pressing against him.

Blondie fell back, grasping at his face, trying to claw off the unseen threat. But Max could see it. The blurs covered Blondie's head like a plastic bag, and as he suffocated, Max was able to breathe again.

Blondie thrashed on the floor, kicking over chairs, and moaning out a desperate attempt for help. Even if he had wanted to, Max could only muster the strength to breathe. Blondie had seen to that.

And with each breath, the blurs and the girl faded from Max's sight. He was returning to the living. His hammering heart slowed even as Blondie's stopped. By the time Max had enough air to stand, Blondie's blue face stared empty-eyed at the stage.

"Thank you," Max said, his throat scratching the words out. He looked to where the little girl had been and smiled. "I can't see you anymore, but if you're here, please, follow me."

Max crossed to the back of the stage where a narrow staircase led to the dressing rooms below. Leaning against the wall as he stumbled down the stairs, he offered a silent wish of thanks to Jules Korner for building such a strange house — he would have fallen down a normal staircase. When he finally reached the main floor, his skin had stopped tingling.

Outside, Sandra took one look at him and rushed from the car. "Are you okay? What happened?" she said as she scooped him up in her arms and kissed him.

"Throat hurts," he managed and then pointed behind him.

He could see by Sandra's reaction that the little girl had followed him out. He waved Sandra on, nodding that he'd be okay, and let her go talk to the girl. The worried gaze she cast his way filled him with warmth.

Max settled in the front passenger's seat and waited. He tried not to think about anything but the paintbrush and the fact that his wife was about to find out its location. He was fooling himself, though. His mind played out those final moments when he saw the blurs, when he had almost died.

A well of tears rushed up. He tried to hold them back, but doing so constricted his throat, sending sharp pains into his chest. So, he buried his face in the crook of his arm and cried. There wasn't any closer to death he could have gone.

When Sandra returned to the car, she had a triumphant look that fell the second she saw her husband. He wiped at his eyes, but he couldn't hide anything. She came to him and wrapped her arms around his body.

"You're okay," she said. "You're alive."

He let out a shaking breath. "Forgive me. All my stupidness."

"Nothing to forgive."

He smiled and kissed her. "Good thing I married you."

Tears flowed again, only this time they belonged to Sandra. Max brought her in close, held her against his chest, and let her sweet scent fill his lungs. Though his body still shook with adrenaline, he knew he'd be okay. As long as she stayed with him.

"I've got it," Drummond said, appearing just a few feet away. "I found Korner. I know now."

Sandra lifted her head with a cocky grin. "I already know. A little dead girl told me."

"Well, I don't know. What are we talking about?" Max said a bit too hard and winced.

Drummond came in close as Sandra took in the air to speak. Together they said, "I know where the paintbrush is."

# Chapter 21

THE OLD HONDA SHIVERED as Sandra pressed the gas pedal further down. Max cringed at the sound of the straining engine, but he didn't say a word. If anything, he wanted Sandra to push the car faster.

Drummond leaned forward from the backseat, his excitement flowing out of him like a faucet opened full. "Jules Korner is one of the nicest ghosts I've ever met. The moment he heard I was looking for him, he started working to find me. Not an easy thing to do when you consider how enormous the Other is and just how many ghosts there are to get through."

Sandra passed an elderly couple in a car that looked a decade older than the Honda. "Well my little girl, Rebecca, she was every bit as nice and helpful. She felt awful about what she saw that bastard do to you, hon."

"Blondie? I'd be dead if she hadn't helped." Max rubbed his throat.

"Don't talk. It'll just make it worse," Sandra said.

Drummond pointed out a speed trap, and Sandra braked until she got to a respectable speed. "I'm glad that little girl helped you, but I got my information from the source. Korner told me that he had had several encounters with Corkille and few of them were pleasant. They weren't the buddies that Corkille suggested. In fact, Korner's pretty sure that Corkille forged a few Durham bulls on a few barns taking money out of Korner's pocket and possibly hurting his reputation."

Sandra scrunched her brow. "So, Corkille never taught Korner?"

"Korner wouldn't admit to it, but he had a funny look about the subject. Besides, he gave Corkille the paintbrush as a gift. In my experience, enemies don't usually give gifts. Best I can figure out, they did some work together long ago and then had a falling out."

Sandra scoffed. "That's putting it mildly."

"Oh?"

"Rebecca died decades before Korner broke ground on that land. Murdered. She's been haunting that area ever since. She told me that Corkille had become a leach to Korner, and that one evening the Korner's threw a large party in their home. At the party, Corkille told the story of Blackbeard and suggested they call upon the pirate's spirit for fun. Séances and such were quite popular at the time. Korner wasn't happy at all but he didn't want to embarrass his guests with his disapproval, so he went along."

"Corkille tricked him," Max rasped.

"Yes, and stop talking. Corkille was trying to find the paintbrush even back then. So he used a summoning-possession spell, bringing forth a spirit and letting it possess Korner, who then painted the result. They called for Blackbeard, but they only got some poor fool who knew the rumors."

Drummond slapped the back of Max's headrest. "Let me guess — he painted *Mourning in Red.*"

"Right. Well, he painted the original piece with the shadowed figure. He painted the woman on top of it later. Anyway, the party ended and Corkille left, but Rebecca told me that things forever changed at Korner's Folly. Some residual piece of that magic stayed with Jules — perhaps the possession had not been a poor fool but actually Blackbeard pretending to be a poor fool. Whatever it was, it drove Jules to find that paintbrush. When he succeeded, he recognized what had become of him and he feared for his soul."

"He also hated Corkille for bringing the spirits into his life."

"Exactly. So, he painted over the original and gave it to Corkille along with all the things associated with the painting — all the paints, the easel, and the brushes."

"Including the paintbrush, right?"

"Right. I think he hoped to break free from whatever magic

surrounded him, but also, I think he secretly wanted to put it onto Corkille as well. Either way, Rebecca said he had Corkille arrive at the Folly one day, handed him the painting and the materials, and explained that this ended their relationship. Howard Corkille was no longer welcome."

"And over the years, the painting got lost," Max said. "Corkille never realized he had the brush the whole time."

"Until now," Drummond said. "Korner told me that he had spoken with a witch who summoned him shortly before he learned that I was looking for him."

"Let me guess."

Sandra hit Max's arm lightly. "Stop talking or I'm going to drop you off at home first."

Drummond said, "Dr. Connor knows the whole story, so you can bet Modesto knows too. My guess is that they sent Blondie to the Folly to wait for you, to stall you, while they went to Corkille to get the paintbrush. If Corkille didn't figure it out on his own, he'll know the second they arrive."

"He knows," Sandra said, getting off the highway. "In fact, he's known from the moment we brought that painting back. He looked at it, figured the whole thing out, and then sent us off to Korner's Folly. But he made sure Melinda stayed behind. He was pretty firm about it. Why? Because he needs her help to find the paintbrush and perform the spell. He definitely knows."

"Sweets, you've got great intuition and reasoning skills. Someday, when you die, think about holding on and becoming a ghost. We could have a great time."

Though Max couldn't speak well, he could still scowl. Sandra caught his reaction from the corner of her eye and let out a snicker. "Sorry, Marshall. I'm all for Max." Max's scowl turned upward into a gloat.

As Sandra neared the Corkille house, all the talk ceased. Max wasn't sure exactly what they would find, but he knew enough to be concerned, and clearly so did the rest of his team. *His team.* He liked the sound of that. More than just a nice sounding concept, he knew it to be true.

Each one of the three of them provided indispensable skills they needed. Take out any one of them, and there would be no way to make this business work. Inwardly, Max marveled at the absurd idea that up until this point he had been trying to find a way to get his wife out of the office.

It had been fear. He knew that now. At first, fear of the financial pressures. Then, Melinda and Howard kept them spinning so much, he feared failing the case and losing any possible momentum that would have on their business.

Thinking of the Corkilles did nothing good for Max. He could feel the fires building in his gut. He knew that sensation all too well lately. But everybody in this case, the Corkilles, Jasper Sullivan, Connor and Modesto, every single one of them lied and manipulated Max and his team over this paintbrush. A damn paintbrush!

"Max?" Sandra said, the false calm in her voice easy to catch. "Are you okay?" She must've noticed his rising anger. If anybody could pick up on that, it would be her.

"Let's just get there," he said, and not another word passed in the car. Even Drummond had the sense to stay quiet.

Max had the car door open before Sandra had even stopped. He stomped up to the front door and kicked it in. A bit over-the-top, he'd admit, but it just felt good.

"Max!" Sandra said, and though he heard her calling, his brain shoved any response aside.

He stormed into the foyer. The house was dark, but with so many windows, a full moon, and the Honda's headlights, Max had no trouble finding his way. He cut into the living room (or maybe they called it the receiving room, who knew with folks like this), tore away the plant hiding the studio door, and pushed in.

"Howard?" he called out. No answer came. He flicked on the lights to find the studio unoccupied.

As Drummond slipped in through the wall, Max whirled around to leave. Sandra blocked the doorway. "Look, honey, I can see you're upset, but we need to approach this sensibly."

Drummond said, "Listen to your wife. I've seen too many cops and PIs end up in the hospital because of going into a situation hot-headed. Just calm down and —"

"Out of my way," Max said and barreled past Sandra.

As he worked toward the kitchen, he opened every door he went by. Closets and entrances to a study or a bathroom or a dining room. Stairs to the basement.

Max stared down that dark chasm for a moment. "Howard? Melinda? You down there?" His voice echoed back. He stood still and listened, raising his hand to stop Sandra and Drummond from making noise.

Drummond cleared his throat, and before Max could scold him, he said, "I'm a ghost. I'll just go down and check it out. Be right back." He slid through the floor and was gone no more than ten seconds. "Nope. Empty down there."

Slamming the basement door, Max stomped to the upstairs. He took one look down the long hall and it hit him. The maids didn't go into the one room, the room that Howard Corkille had been living in for more decades than was natural, the Other Room.

Picking up his pace, the grin of a hunter on his face, Max headed straight for the end of the hall. The dark, wooden door had been left ajar. Max burst through, hoping to catch them or surprise whomever might be left, only to find another empty room. Nothing but a bed and that chair facing out the window.

"Damn," he said as Sandra and Drummond came in behind him. "They have to be here. Corkille's too old, too frail, to be moved around. He could barely make it down to his studio."

"We've been gone all day," Sandra said. "Maybe they just took their time moving. Maybe they're far from here."

"No. If they aren't here, then Connor and Modesto got to them. We're too late." Max dropped onto the edge of the bed and rubbed his face. "They've got to be here. I can feel it."

Sandra looked to Drummond. "Go check the rest of the house. See what you can find."

"I'll try," Drummond said with a defeated tone. "Don't

expect much, though, and don't think it'll be quick. This place is like Korner's Folly with all its little rooms."

Max lifted his head, more alert suddenly. Something was different. He looked around the room, trying to recall the day he found Howard Corkille. Sandra, bless her, stayed quiet and watched carefully while Drummond left to search the other rooms.

*I came in and saw Corkille sitting there,* Max thought. He wanted to speak, he thought best when he did so out loud, but his throat wouldn't allow it. Breathing hurt enough, let alone speaking. He didn't look forward to eating anytime soon.

He walked around the room, pointing to different objects until he saw the bedroom's back corner. That was it. A Japanese tri-fold screen had been set-up there before.

Max approached the corner with cautious steps. He pressed his ear against the wall. A muted sound drifted upward like a ghostly moan, both quiet and disturbing.

Stepping back, Max inspected the wall — dirty, brown wall paper above a chair rail and wood panels below. "There," he said despite the pain and pointed at one wood panel. With a gentle touch, he pressed and pulled on the panel trying to figure out how it opened.

Sandra had been watching him this whole time. Crouching next to him, she placed her hand on the panel and slid it to the side. It opened with ease.

She shrugged. "Lucky guess."

Max stuck his head into the wall and looked around. Nothing special. Just wood and wires, dust and dirt. But he could hear that moaning voice more clearly now.

He pulled his head out and thrust his arm in, feeling around. *There's got to be some kind of* — Click. His hand passed over a switch and on the adjacent wall making up the corner, a full-sized door opened.

Max and Sandra looked at each other. "Careful," Max whispered.

"You, too," she said.

Max took one step toward the door when Sandra grabbed

his shoulders and kissed him. At first, they pressed hard against each other but then eased back enough to feel lip against lip. It wasn't a sensual kiss. It didn't arouse thoughts of the bedroom. Rather, the kiss filled Max with memories of all the wonderful moments in his life he owed to Sandra. The kiss pulled from him the deep-seated love that made up the core of his being. He could feel his heart bursting for his wife. And just when the thought hit him that should anything bad happen, this could be their last kiss, he understood that she had figured that much out already.

They let go, smiled, and headed through the door. A few feet in, the floor gave way to a narrow staircase. It went down the inside of the house, perhaps riding underneath the original stairwell, perhaps hidden between walls nobody noticed to be too thick. It was a forgery of architecture that traveled below the first floor into a second, separate basement.

As they neared the bottom, the fluttering glow of candlelight lit the way. That awful moaning continued. The closer they came, the more Max could hear that the sound actually came from two different sources. One was a woman's voice, chanting in a long, mournful tone. The other was of a person in pain.

When they reached the basement, both Max and Sandra jumped back in surprise. The room was a large square with a low ceiling. A chalk circle had been drawn on the concrete floor and around the ring were symbols like those found in Dr. Connor's books. Candles lined the cinderblock walls.

Howard Corkille sat in the center of the circle, wearing a white cloth as if he thought himself to be a monk or Gandhi. But one look at the far wall showed his lack of compassion. Dr. Connor and Mr. Modesto stood with their arms chained to the beams above their heads.

Max had just enough time to take this in. Melinda Corkille, dressed in a black cloak, stepped in front of him and raised her hand.

"Always causing trouble," she said and sprayed something in his face. As she waved the spray into Sandra's direction, Max felt the world slip away.

# Chapter 22

BEFORE MAX COULD OPEN HIS EYES, he felt pain. His throat stung as if he had a sunburn on the inside; his right hip throbbed as if he had fallen on a concrete sidewalk; his shoulders and arms burned as if two giants played tug-of-war with him as the rope. Everything hurt. He heard Sandra moan nearby and tried to open his eyes.

At first, no luck. Whatever Melinda had sprayed in their faces had left a sticky crust around his eyelids. He tried to wipe it away only to discover that his hands were handcuffed over his head. Thankfully, he wasn't hanging that way other than from being unconscious. Planting his feet on the ground relieved the stress on his shoulders, arms, and wrists though the pain remained.

While trying to stretch his eyebrows high, he managed to crack one eyelid open, then the other. Though he only saw through a crusty residue, he could make out the room and the situation. It wasn't good.

They were still in the secret chamber with the circle, the candles, and the Corkilles. Sandra, Max, Dr. Connor, and Mr. Modesto had been handcuffed to pipes on the ceiling. They were spread out to four points on the circle that, if connected, would form a huge X. Howard still occupied the center (where the X would intersect) and Melinda, dressed in a dark cloak and little else, walked the inner part of the circle while chanting softly to herself.

"Max?" Sandra said, groggy and sore.

Melinda halted her march, tilted her head toward Sandra, and licked her lips. "No, no, foolish girl. Max is of no use to you anymore." She walked the circle again. "None of you can help each other nor yourselves." She stopped at Dr. Connor who looked weak and defeated. "Not even you."

Mr. Modesto held on to a modicum of pride, standing firm and tall despite his chains and bruised face. "You are the foolish girl if you honestly believe that a man like Mr. Hull will let you —"

"Let me? Mr. Hull? You are so naïve it's a bit sad, really. Mr. Hull has had no power in this from the beginning. While you and your witch here spent all your time trying to weasel back into the Hull family's grace, do you really think Terrance Hull had no clue? Let me? No. He *let you* run around like fools. He used you as pawns so he could get to the magic that he sought. And the only reason that he bothered with you at all was so he could get Max to do the work."

"What?" Sandra said as if Melinda's words were smelling salts.

"Good, she's awake." With a triumphant strut, Melinda approached Sandra. "Time to face the hard truth. Your husband would never work for Hull. Hull knows that. So how else could he get Max to put his charming, diligent talents to use? Hull let word slip to his bumbling, idiot cronies that he sought a certain painting, that it was of great power and importance, and that he would reward his people well for finding it.

"Modesto and his witch are not subtle. Hull knows this. He counted on it. He figured that word would get to Max eventually — after all," she said, looking at Max over her shoulder, letting the curve of her breast show just beyond the cloak, "you're the only one around here who really deals with these kinds of investigations."

Max thought of Jasper Sullivan. Hull had put out the word like chum and simply waited for a shark like Sullivan to arrive. Max didn't doubt it to be true. People like Hull and Corkille, people who know about ghosts and magic, they know they are always surrounded by otherworldly things. For another person, the whole plan would be ridiculous, but for Hull — especially considering the vast, spider web of connections the Hull family had created in the area over the centuries — it wasn't hard to believe. Hull knew Corkille had enough enemies over two centuries that someone, alive or dead, would take interest and hire the only man working the magic angle — Max. And if no one had taken the bait, Hull surely had a back-up plan, probably more direct, probably something Max would have hated more.

Looking up at his hands cuffed to a pipe, Max thought, *Hated more than this?*

At the foot of each captive, Melinda had drawn a symbol in chalk. "You people — you're all just pawns. You think you're smart or brave or ahead of everyone else. You're nothing. This fight has always been between the Corkilles and the Hulls, and tonight the Corkilles will finally win. Howard will be released from his dread curse, Blackbeard's magic will be used up in the process, and without that, Hull won't be able to raise his abominable ancestors."

Dr. Connor cringed. "And all that power released — the curse, the voodoo — all of that magic — you won't let it just dissipate into the air, right?"

Melinda arched an eyebrow. "That would be wasteful, and we must strive to be green, mustn't we? No, I think it best if I absorb all of that power. I think this city needs to be rid of the Hulls. And when I have that power, well, a little revenge would taste good, too."

Dr. Connor's face returned to the maniacal drunk Max had encountered on a few days ago. "You're a moronic dolt," she said. "Terrance Hull will destroy you and barely lift his pinkie."

"If you believe that, then you don't understand the great power infused in the brush." Melinda patted the side of her cloak.

"But you don't know Terrance Hull. You think we're surprised that he used us? You think we feel betrayed or even offended? He's supposed to use us. I'm nothing more than a tool for this great man from a great family to use however he sees fit. You should be afraid, little girl. Ask Max. He knows just how hard it is to go against the Hulls."

Melinda whirled to Max, letting her cloak flow back over her shoulders, letting Max see her firm breasts, her flat stomach, her smooth hips. "I can't say I care much at all for what Max Porter thinks. He could've had me. Look at this body. You gave this up?"

Max locked eyes with Sandra. "I love my wife." Sandra's lips trembled a kiss in the air.

Melinda stepped between them. "Aw, isn't that sweet. But so stupid, too. You should've slept with me when I had offered. Then this would've been avoidable. See, Blackbeard's hair may be infused with that voodoo priestess's spell, but it needs a catalyst to get hold of all that power. That catalyst is the life essence. Perhaps Dr. Connor would explain what that is?"

Dr. Connor snarled. "Rot in Hell."

"She's a bit out of sorts," Melinda said, shrugging one shoulder. "Oh well, I've had to do it all myself this long, might as well keep going." She stepped closer to Max, the tips of her breasts brushing his chest. "The life essence is simply any bodily fluid that carries your life. Had you slept with me, I would already have your fluids and you wouldn't be here."

Max looked beyond toward Sandra. "Happy to disappoint."

Melinda's hand moved fast, slapping Max's cheek with surprising force. "Pay attention. Just because you turned away from what would have been the best lay of your life doesn't mean I don't win. You could have had a wonderful afternoon of pleasures your wife can't even begin to imagine. She probably hasn't even heard of half the techniques I know. Instead, you get this. Because there are other life essence fluids in the body. Blood, for example."

Her words died against the low ceiling, leaving the room in cold silence. She stepped back, offering Max one final view of her tone body before pulling the cloak back over. "Let's start proper," she said and faced Mr. Modesto. "No one is more proper than you. At least, no one pretends to be more proper, especially when serving out the most despicable orders."

Despite his bruised cheek and bleeding lip, Modesto raised his chin and managed to exude a small portion of dignity. "It is no wonder that Mr. Porter declined your advances. You're a hideous person."

In a flash, Melinda snatched a simple, wooden bowl and an elaborate dagger from a recess in the wall. She cracked Modesto across his proud chin with the blade's hilt. Max saw Modesto's eyes roll but he came back a moment later. Just in time to watch as Melinda sliced a line open on his chest.

She didn't bother opening his shirt. She let the sharp blade do all the work. Shirt and skin cut open with ease, and a patch of blood spread.

After setting the dagger down, she ripped the cut shirt off. The bowl came next. She placed it against Modesto's chest and pushed on the wound to release more blood. As it collected in the bowl, slowly dribbling like syrup, Melinda whispered foreign words. Max tried to hear her, but he couldn't make sense of it.

He looked everywhere, twisting his wrists around the handcuffs only to find the block wall behind him. Melinda lowered the bowl on the circle's edge, dipped her finger in the blood, and traced the chalk symbols she had drawn earlier. With his foot, Max rubbed an opening in the circle, and while he did disturb the chalk, he uncovered lines that had been painted on the floor. As Melinda rose with the bowl and dagger and headed toward Dr. Connor, Max tried to clear his mind, not to panic, and to find a way out.

"Your usefulness to the Hull family has long since run its course," Melinda said as Dr. Connor glared at her in defiance, "and I can guarantee that I'll have no use for you when the Corkille family takes over. But, if it gives you any comfort, you'll have one final use, and it'll be for this spell."

Snarling, Melinda jabbed the dagger into Dr. Connor's stomach and placed the bowl underneath to catch the blood. The witch grunted and sweat beaded on her forehead, but she managed not to scream.

"Stop this," Modesto said, his voice weakening. "I'm sure we can make a deal."

"Is that right?" Melinda shook her head. "You have some great pull with the Hulls that I don't know about? Even if you did, why would the Hulls deal with me — the woman who will usurp them? Oh, look, I think Dr. Connor is trying to be brave."

To Max's utter shock, Dr. Connor maintained her firm glare on Melinda as if to say, *You'll never beat me.* Melinda jabbed the dagger into the witch once more. Dr. Connor barely reacted. She held her witch's gaze until her eyes lost focus and her head slumped forward.

Modesto let out a whimper while as before, Melinda whispered odd words and then knelt on the circle. She traced the chalk symbols with blood as she continued this strange rite. Max saw Modesto lose control. The once-dignified man kicked and screamed and cried. He tried to free himself but without success.

Each burst of energy lessened in strength from the previous one. It was a strange thing to watch. Max could actually see the moment that Modesto gave up. It held for just a second. One moment, Modesto railed against his bonds and spitted out his hatred for Melinda. Then, for a flashing instant, he froze. Max saw it in his eyes — the acceptance of fate. The next moment, Modesto let his body hang as he wept in silence.

Melinda ignored Modesto as if he were a child acting up for a parent's attention. When she had finished her blood tracings, she rose with the dagger and bowl in hand and turned toward Sandra.

"No," Max said, his body flushing with cold fear.

Melinda watched Max from the corner of her eye as she crossed the room. "It's too bad your sweetheart isn't more awake. I guess I drugged her a bit too much. It would've been fun to listen to her scream. And you, too."

Though tears streamed down his face, Max held his tongue. He looked around the room again, desperate to find anything useful. But he saw nothing that he could reach. Not with his hands cuffed to the pipe above him.

"Still," Melinda continued, "I don't need her to be awake. I simply need to take her blood."

"No!" Max cried out.

"Don't worry. I'll slit her wrists so the blood drains slowly. That way you can watch her death for a long, painful time."

Max yanked against the pipe. With every muscle, every bit of strength he could summon, he let out a garbled cry, his damaged throat scalding pain straight up to his teeth, and he pulled down hard. The pipe didn't appear to budge, but he continued to pull.

"Say goodbye to your love," Melinda said and slashed the dagger across Sandra's wrist.

"Ouch," Sandra said in a distant voice.

Max's eyes widened and he doubled his efforts. Dust sifted off the pipe, drifting onto his face. Melinda raised her bowl to gather the blood and whisper her words.

Furiously, Max yanked down. Over and over. Each time the pipe shook but did not break loose.

When Melinda knelt on the circle and began her tracings, Max screamed out and gave all he could into breaking that pipe. Still, it remained intact.

Melinda stood, gathered her bowl and dagger, and looked upon Max like a lover finally getting her man. Panting, Max looked back with such hatred, Melinda hesitated.

"Oh, now," she said, "don't be that way." She opened her cloak once more and sauntered toward him. Biting her bottom lip, she traced her breast with the tip of the dagger leaving behind a dotted trail of blood. "It's not too late, you know. Mmmm. I think we could have a good time." She placed a hand on his chest and licked his neck. Her hand slid down until it rested between his legs. "Maybe I should coax that other fluid from you while you watch your wife dying across the room."

Max spit on her. "There's a fluid for you."

Rage flashed in Melinda's eyes. Her mouth turned down and she stabbed the dagger at his groin. She looked down. "I missed," she said, pulling the blade from his thigh. "Guess it's your lucky day. You might even get to die before your wife."

While Melinda let Max's blood fill her bowl, she kept her eyes locked on his face. Max felt his blood flow out but he refused to look down. He just watched her and waited. He knew what was about to happen. He waited for it. His only chance.

With the bowl filled, Melinda kissed Max's cheek and turned around to face the circle. This was it. Max pulled himself upward on the pipe and lifted his legs toward her shoulders. He had hoped to wrap his legs around her neck, but he was too weak now to get his legs high enough. He did manage to kick her in the back, sending her stumbling into the circle.

Melinda let out a screech of surprise as she fell to one knee. All her focus shifted to keeping the blood from spilling out of the bowl. Her body shook as she gently placed the bowl on the floor. Then she let out a huge sigh.

"That's why I like you," she said, turning to Max. "You don't give up, do you? But you failed. Not a drop spilled."

"Come back and I'll try again."

Melinda picked up the bowl and stood straight. "I am coming back, and I'm going to finish this spell. If you try anything again, I'll walk over to your beloved Sandra and slit her neck. You understand? She's dying right now, but she's not dead yet. Who knows? Maybe when I'm done with this, I'll let her live. But if you do anything more to disrupt me, you'll be responsible for her guaranteed death. Am I clear?"

Though Max shook with anger, though his eyes blazed his frustration, though his fingers curled into fists, he nodded.

"Good," Melinda said, approaching as before. This time, as she turned toward the circle, she paused long enough to send Max a warning glance. He refused to meet her eyes. She knelt on the circle and completed tracing the symbols in blood.

"Now," she said, "it's time." She stepped into the circle and knelt right behind Howard Corkille. Like a seasoned caregiver, she eased him back, reclining his body until his head rested in her lap.

"Thank you," Howard said, his words shaky and cracking. "Thank you all for the sacrifice you are making for me. I'm so tired of this world. But to know that my darling Melinda will benefit in such an enormous way makes this parting all that much better."

"Shhh," Melinda said, stroking Howard's head. "It's time for you to finally rest."

"Yes. Rest. That sounds wonderful."

Howard closed his eyes and Melinda lifted her hands upward. She started to moan in low, drawn-out tones like an ancient monk deep in meditation. The only break came when she drew breath.

"Boy-o-boy, that's horrible," Drummond said as he lowered through the ceiling. "I can hear her through the floorboards."

"Where the hell have you been?" Max said despite the hot pain in his throat and the deep relief he felt the moment he saw the old ghost. Modesto looked up, his brow scrunched, but he said nothing.

Drummond raised his hands. "Sorry. I got lost. Y'know, I think old Jules Korner must've helped design this place. It's a darn maze." After a quick survey of the room, he added, "Doesn't look like things are going all that well for you."

"Shut up and do something," Max said.

"Like what?"

"Like stick your hand into her head and stop all this." Max's face puckered at the pain in his throat.

"Kill her? Doesn't look like things are that bad."

Max's face found enough blood to turn red. "Sandra is dying," he managed. He tasted the bitter copper of blood in his mouth.

Drummond swooped in on Sandra. "Can you hear me?"

Sandra raised an eye. She looked pale and weak.

"Sorry, Max," Drummond said. "I didn't realize it was so serious. I'll take care of everything."

Puffing out his chest, Drummond slid forward, his arms reaching out toward Melinda's head. But when he hit the circle's edge, he screamed out and fell backward. Light tendrils of smoke twined above him.

Melinda paused her moaning chant long enough to laugh. "Sorry. No ghosts allowed."

With one hand rubbing his head, Drummond said, "That hurt."

Melinda watched Max as she rose to her feet. Her eyes widened, her mouth leered, her expression twisted — she was a gargoyle celebrating freedom from its stony prison. "The time has arrived," she said. "I won't be just an obedient little girl anymore. I won't be a caretaker for a fossilized man. Soon, I will have the power to change everything."

She lifted her right hand, and Max saw the paintbrush clenched in her fingers. It was small, pencil thin, the kind of brush used for fine, detailed work. Max marveled at the sight. All this trouble caused over a few hairs on this tiny brush.

"Now," Melinda said turning toward Howard's sleeping body, "you will no longer suffer."

"Drummond," Max whispered softly both to protect his damaged throat and to keep Melinda from hearing. "You have to save Sandra. Nothing else matters to me. Okay?"

For all his sarcasm and foolishness, the core of Marshall Drummond came out when needed the most. The ghost took one look at Max, gave one understanding nod, and whisked across the room. He placed both hands around Sandra's wrist and closed his eyes in concentration.

Her hand turned white as a supernatural cold infiltrated her skin. The blood stopped flowing from her wrist. Sandra's eyes snapped open as the cold shocked her awake. She looked around, confused and desperate to comprehend.

The air inside the circle shimmered and warped around the Corkilles. Max tried to watch Sandra, but the air between them twisted her image as if looking through a glass of water.

"Max," Sandra called out. "Max, I'm okay. Dizzy, but okay."

He wanted to let her know he was fine. He wanted to scream out how much he loved her. But he only had a few more words in him before his throat refused to make any sound until it healed. He thought he should hold on to them.

Melinda held the brush over Howard's body. In a bright flash, the hairs on the brush ignited, burning hotter and higher than should have been possible. Max squinted against the light, but he could still see what happened.

Howard Corkille's arms jerked to the side. Then his legs.

Then his entire body spasmed on the floor as if suffering seizures.

"By the blood of those surrounding," Melinda said, "Free this man from that which binds him."

Max couldn't say what he expected to occur, but there was no huge light show, no swirling of spirits, no cracking of the curse. Instead, the air stopped shimmering and the flaming brush lowered to a burning ember. Howard's body settled.

The old man lifted his hand toward Melinda, and his mouth opened into a toothy grin. "I'm free," he said. And his hand flopped to floor. His body empty. Howard Corkille was dead.

Max looked up from the body and saw his wife staring back at him. His eyes glistened as she blew him a kiss. But a frown took over her expression as her eyes focused just above Melinda's head.

"Can you see this?" she asked.

He peered in the same direction, but he saw nothing.

"He can't see it," Drummond said.

"There's an energy above her. It's not like a ghost. It's something strange," Sandra said.

A soft pop of air startled Melinda as the brush ignited once more. The flame no longer hurt to see but it had an odd tinge of purple and blue inside it. It flickered in the air and lit Melinda's face from beneath creating harsh, ugly shadows.

"By the soul of Edward Teach, Blackbeard the Pirate," Melinda said, raising her hands toward the invisible force above her. "By the infinite powers of the great voodoo priestesses of old, I call upon you to take this broken curse, consume its energy, consume its centuries of power, all that it was which now rests in this token of your power —" She shook the brush as if the power would dash from it and sprinkle down.

To the side, Max saw Dr. Connor moving her head. It took a lot of effort but she managed to look right at Max. Her mouth moved but Max couldn't hear her above Melinda's spell casting.

"Dump the bowl!" Sandra said. "Connor says to dump the bowl."

Max nodded and moved his foot toward the bowl of his own blood. Though he stretched as far as his sore limbs would permit, the bowl remained out of reach. Melinda had been careful.

"— take it all from here and release it back unto me. Come into me, spirits of the past, so I may rule as you would once have wanted to rule."

Pointing at Melinda with his free hand, Drummond said, "That woman is nuts."

"Come into me. Come into me," Melinda chanted.

Sandra's face paled, and at first Max thought Drummond had put his ghostly touch on her for too long. Then she said, "Max ... I don't believe it. I think I'm seeing Blackbeard's ghost."

# Chapter 23

"COME INTO ME," Melinda said. "I am an open vessel."

Max pulled down on the cuffs, but he knew nothing would come of it. He needed to do something, though. He looked around the room, hoping to find some miracle item that he hadn't noticed before.

He saw Dr. Connor, head hung low, her body devoid of any energy. Modesto watched the circle with an expression equal parts disdain and defeat. Sandra stared at an empty space which, no doubt, contained the apparition of Blackbeard. Drummond, holding Sandra's wrist, also looked upon the pirate ghost.

*We're a sorry bunch,* Max thought.

"Come," Melinda continued, and waved the smoldering brush in front of her like incense. She reached out with her free hand, and though Max could not see Blackbeard, he pictured the pirate taking her hand like a gentleman asking to dance. But then her body jolted and her twisted face grimaced.

"He's got her," Sandra said. "He's got her."

Whatever pain Melinda had felt, sifted away. Her face softened with a blissful calm. She lifted her eyes toward Max, and looking more sadistic than Max had ever encountered before, she picked up the dagger. "Not enough blood," she said, her voice having dropped an octave. She was no longer Melinda. Blackbeard had control.

She looked down at Howard Corkille and cut open his wrist. Like a vampire, she brought the wrist to her mouth. A little blood pooled but without his heart pumping, there was no flow.

She threw Howard's wrist to the floor and let out an angry grunt. "Need more," she said, and it occurred to Max that the second part of this spell, the part intended to give Melinda such great power, may not have worked entirely. She had said that life fluids were important, but she never said just how important.

Max looked at Howard's corpse. That blood was no good. Howard only provided dead fluids now. So why wasn't Blackbeard/Melinda coming after them, the living, cutting them open?

Max's lips turned up in a devilish grin. Blackbeard may be in Melinda's body, but for now, he was still a ghost. He couldn't get out of the circle any more than Drummond could get in.

Thinking of Drummond and his ghostliness brought another thought to Max like a shining sun bursting through a terrible storm. Knowing his throat would hate him for more talking, Max braced himself for the pain that would come, and said, "Honey, trust me."

Sandra looked right at Max, straight into his heart. "Always."

"Drummond, let go of her wrist and come over here."

Drummond hesitated. "The cold won't last long without me."

"I know," Max said.

"She'll start to bleed again."

Sandra shook her arms. "Trust him, already."

Drummond looked from wife to husband and back. "If you start to get light-headed, you yell for me. I'll run right back."

As Drummond went around the circle to cross the room, Melinda tried to reach out toward Dr. Connor. The circle prevented her from touching the witch. She spotted the blood-traced symbols on the floor, and like a famished wildcat, she dropped on all fours, and licked what hadn't dried yet.

"What now?" Drummond asked as he approached Max.

"Put your hands on the chain between my handcuffs. You freeze it like you did Sandra's wrist, only I want you to put everything into it. I want that chain so cold that it's practically ice itself. Can you do that?" Max said, his voice fading into a whisper at the end.

Drummond nodded. He placed his hand on the chain,

closed his eyes, and touched the metal. Max could see the pain this caused. Touching the corporeal world always caused pain. But, if nothing else, Drummond had always been a tough detective. He winced, bared his teeth, and grunted, but he never cried out.

Melinda scrabbled toward the bloody symbols near Modesto. When she finished there, she moved on to Sandra's symbols. Every so often, she reached toward the circle's edge with one hand. Each time, she pulled it back as if stung. Except Max noticed that each time, she kept her hand against the barrier a little longer. Instinct told Max that when she finished all the blood the symbols had, it would be enough to free her from the circle.

He yanked downward. "Colder," he said.

Melinda looked up. Max could tell by her gaze that she now saw Drummond. A benefit of having Blackbeard inside her, he guessed. Understanding crossed her face, and she sped up her ingestion of the blood.

"Hurry," Max said.

Drummond put both hands on the chain. "Keep trying," he said.

As Max pulled down, Melinda rushed across to the bloody symbols at his feet. She lapped it up, laughing at Max's desperation.

"I'm going to have fun killing you," she said.

He inhaled deeply and put every ounce of strength he had into one crushing pull. His wrists screamed out as the cuffs dug into his skin, but then he tumbled to the ground and little pieces of frozen metal tinkled on the floor. Drummond floated backward, his eyes closed in relief.

"Max!" Sandra screamed.

As he faced her, Melinda stepped out of the circle and backhanded him across the cheek. Not only had Blackbeard giving her the ability to see the dead, but Max learned that she also had gained a lot of his brute strength. The blow to his face sent Max rolling across the floor.

Max stumbled to his feet just as Melinda rushed him. She

grabbed his shirt and shoved him against the wall. She punched him in the gut. He doubled over, his lungs giving up all their air, his eyes watering at the pain. Bile raced up, burning the sore tissue as it coated his throat. He struggled to remain standing.

Melinda clasped his chin in her hand and forced his head upward. She gazed down upon him, and Max glimpsed the pirate inside her. He had heard that Blackbeard struck fear in the men he fought against, and Max understood why. The fierce eyes blazing at him lacked compassion, humanity, or even sanity. Had Melinda succeeded, she would have had great power. But with Blackbeard controlling Melinda, her power was vicious.

She pulled back a fist and slammed it across his temple. Max dropped to the ground. The world spun around him.

He thought he heard Sandra screaming his name, but her voice sounded muffled and dazed. He turned his head toward her. The floor rushed up to his face, cold and hard.

He saw a figure stand over him. A dark, shadowed figure. Blackbeard. The pirate raised one, powerful foot.

"Goodbye, Max Porter," a voice said.

But that foot never slammed down. The pain never came. Instead, the shadowed figure arched back and toppled over with a surprised yell.

Max rolled onto his side to see what had happened. The first thing he discerned through his blurred vision was that the fallen figure belonged to Melinda Corkille. That made sense and helped clear his muddled brain. The second thing he saw was Drummond floating above Melinda.

Drummond turned his head toward Max and nodded. He shouldn't have done so. Melinda's hand shot upward and smashed Drummond toward the ceiling.

"Idiot," she said. "I am the great Blackbeard. I can see you, and I can touch you, and I most certainly can destroy you."

Melinda clamored to her feet and swung out with her fists. Drummond moved fast, though, and with the grace of an experienced fighter. He dodged her punches and countered with two strong jabs that popped hard, stumbling her back a few steps. Without Blackbeard coursing thorough her, Max figured Melinda would've been out cold.

Back and forth Melinda and Drummond traded blows. Max watched from the floor, his body slowly recuperating. He could see one solid image instead of blurred doubles, and he could breathe without hot pokers attacking his lungs. Swallowing still hurt, but then he fully expected to be on an all-liquid diet for the next few weeks.

Drummond dashed to the right, avoiding Melinda's left fist. He grabbed her near the elbow and swung her around. She fell into Modesto who made no effort to kick out — he was unconscious.

Melinda lunged for Drummond, caught him by the leg, and took him down to the floor. She straddled him, pinning his arms down with her knees, and punched him in the face. Over and over, she connected.

Max had been watching the fight fully expecting Drummond to win. But now things had turned ugly. He rolled up onto all fours, held the position a moment until his stomach settled back, and crawled toward the fight. He had no illusions that he could hurt Melinda in his condition, but he did hope to distract her long enough for Drummond to get free.

She spotted him out of the corner of her eye. "Naughty, naughty," she said, but she took the bait. She reached toward him, perhaps planning to shove him away.

Max had enough strength to latch onto her wrist and fall down. His weight yanked her off balance. Like a bird freed from its cage, Drummond shot into the air, curved around, and knocked Melinda to the side. She fought back, but the two were on even ground again.

"Max," Sandra said, calling him from far away. No. Near. His ears could hear her so closely. He inched his head upward and saw that he had moved quite close to his wife.

"The bowl," she said. "Connor said to knock over the bowl."

Like a drunkard, Max lolled to his side. Ahead of him was the bowl Melinda had used to collect their blood. He stared at it, trying to will his body to move. He was so tired, so weakened. He wanted to close his eyes and sleep.

"Hurry!" Drummond yelled as Melinda tossed him against the stairs. He shot back at her but she parried his attacks.

Max crawled his arm in the direction of the bowl. He felt heat radiating from it. Pushing with his feet, he scooted closer until his fingers made contact. The bowl's surface was rougher than he had expected.

"Turn it over," Sandra said. "You've almost got it."

Melinda's head snapped around. "No!" She darted toward Max but Drummond jumped onto her back, wrapped his arm around her throat, and pulled her away. With a lazy smile, Max flipped the bowl closer toward himself.

Nothing happened.

"Sorry," Max whispered. Too tired to go on, Max let his arm flop downward. It hit the bowl, cracking it into three pieces.

Flames, purple and blue like those from the brush, snaked out of the bowl's shards. Drummond shoved Melinda toward the center of the circle. Like a child lost in a store, Melinda looked from face to face, hoping one would be her salvation.

The flames rose higher, weaving in a hypnotic rhythm. If they had eyes, Max would have sworn they were staring at Melinda. Whatever they burned on — chalk, blood, concrete, or the supernatural — the odor rivaled any natural gas leak Max had experienced. He coughed at the horrible smell.

Melinda lifted one hand toward Max, and in a voice that was all her own, that lacked any trace of Blackbeard, she said, "It wasn't supposed to be this way." Then the flames speared her.

As she screamed, Max passed out.

# Chapter 24

HOURS LATER, AS THE DAY began beneath his office window, Max settled in his chair and stared at the shot of whiskey on his desk. Sandra had already downed two shots and had prepared a third. Drummond floated by the bookcase, uncharacteristically quiet.

"You going to have that?" Sandra asked.

Max shook his head. He wanted it. He needed it. But he had no doubt that alcohol would light his throat on fire even as it relaxed his frazzled nerves.

His cell phone rang. A glance at the screen told him what he suspected — Mother. Who else would call at the most inappropriate, inconvenient time? He remembered promising her that he would call her back, but if she heard his voice, she'd be on a plane to come nurse him. Probably throw in a few barbs at Sandra while she was at it.

Max pushed the phone across his desk toward Sandra. She looked at the ID and shook her head. "Let it go to voicemail," she said.

When the phone stopped ringing, Drummond said, "You know you can't go to the police."

"Don't we have to?" Sandra asked.

"All that was left of Melinda and Howard were two piles of very fine ash. Everything in that circle turned to ash. You have no bodies, no evidence, no way of proving your story, which — you have to admit — is going to be a tough one for them to swallow as it is. And then there's the tricky aspect that if they believe any of it, they could easily turn the whole thing around to implicate both of you. So, sweetheart, I appreciate you wanting to be honest and forthright, but face it, no cops on this one."

Sandra took Max's shot glass and stared at her wrist wrapped in some yellowed gauze from their inadequate first aid kit. "We should at least go to the hospital."

Max shook his head and pointed to Drummond.

"Honey," Sandra said, "doctors aren't the police."

Drummond slid toward the desk. "I'm afraid Max's right. You can't go to the hospital. They'd take care of him, but they'd also ask a lot of questions. No matter what story you come up with, they're going to notice that the bruises on his neck look like a man being choked to death. Answer the questions, don't answer the questions — either way, the docs are going to notify the police. Then you're back to dealing with the law again."

"We can't do nothing. Max's throat needs serious, professional attention. And my wrist needs stitches, at the least."

"Stitches that'll probably get you locked on a psych ward for a suicide watch."

"Then what do you suggest we do?" Sandra said, her frustration expressing Max's silent anger quite well.

A knock came at the office door which stood open. Mr. Modesto filled the doorway. "Perhaps I can help," he said.

On the surface, Max thought the man looked good. Fresh clothing, a deep shower, and some cologne had wiped away any visible sign of the trauma Modesto had endured. He stepped into the office, his walk formal, his back stiff, his arrogant demeanor all too familiar. Only the moment after he sat near the desk, the moment when his breathing strained and he unconsciously rubbed at his chest, revealed anything improper.

"Perhaps I should be more clear," Modesto said, setting a thin manila envelope on the desk. "I, once again, am in the employ of the Hull family."

Sandra downed the shot of whiskey. "Oh, really? And how are we supposed to believe you this time?"

"Because Mr. Hull is going to take care of everything in a way that is far beyond my meager abilities." Modesto snapped his fingers and a portly, balding man entered. He had a small, black bag at his side, and he headed straight for Max.

"Just these two?" the man asked.

Modesto nodded before continuing. "This man is Dr. Zach Goldman. He is Mr. Hull's personal physician. He will tend to you both right now."

As Modesto spoke, Dr. Goldman treated Max with delicate hands and more care than Max had ever come across in the health care world. He hated to admit it, but the idea of Mr. Hull's doctor working on him gave Max a greater sense of security and confidence than had they gone to the hospital. After all, should the doctor screw up and kill Max, Hull's secret journals would become public knowledge. *Far better,* Max thought, *than any health insurance coverage.*

"Now," Modesto went on, "Mr. Hull has used his formidable connections to ensure there will be no police investigations into any of the matters that have occurred over the course of this situation. Not the Corkilles, not Jasper Sullivan, not the painting, not Jules Korner, not the Welcome Center shooting, not even the tortured postal worker. As far as the police are concerned, all these incidents no longer exist."

"You've got to be kidding," Sandra said, her mouth agape. "I mean I know that the Hull family is powerful, but—"

"The Hull family has always had more ability in this city than you or your thankfully mute husband ever understood."

Drummond snickered. "Only mute for a little while, pal." Max and Sandra joined in for a chuckle.

Modesto sat straighter, ruffled by the reaction. "Regardless, Mr. Hull has also arranged to purchase the Corkille estate and all of its contents. So you needn't fear the discovery of the forgery studio or" — Modesto shuddered — "that other place we were in."

Sandra opened the book with the bottle of whiskey inside. "You want a drink?"

"No, thank you," Modesto said, but his eyes lingered on the bottle. "Furthermore, Mr. Hull wants you to know that although Ms. Corkille used the brush, not all of it was burned to ash. Mr. Hull has possession of the brush and has his top men working on retrieving a usable hair. For the spell he wishes to cast, all he requires is one. Or so Dr. Connor assures. Yes, she'll be fine. Physically."

Cringing as he leaned forward, Modesto pushed the manila enveloped toward Max. "There is one final matter. While Mr. Hull wishes for you to know that he fully recognizes the security you enjoy because of your possession of a copy of his family journal, he also hopes you now see that he has a new card to play in this game — the police."

"Now, hold on," Sandra said, but Max raised a hand to stop her.

"Please, let me speak," Modesto said as Dr. Goldman finished tending Max, wrote down some instructions so as not to disturb Mr. Modesto, and moved on to Sandra. "Mr. Hull has no intention of involving the police in your lives. He merely wants you to understand that holding the journal hostage will only get you so far, and that should you cross that line, Mr. Hull has tremendous resources at his disposal with which to make your lives uncomfortable. Therefore, Mr. Hull would like to form a new arrangement with you."

"Oh, crap, this doesn't sound good," Drummond said.

"From this day forward, the Hull family wishes to pay you a handsome fee in return for keeping you on retainer. You will be free to pursue any other cases you wish, and Mr. Hull promises that you will only be called upon for matters regarding your unique talents — those that are supernatural, if you will. All the finer points are detailed in there," Modesto said, nodding to the envelope.

Though Dr. Goldman fidgeted with her wrist, Sandra stood up — her face red, her body swaying slightly, her breath heavy with whiskey. "You're saying that we have to be at Mr. Hull's beck and call whenever he feels the need to deal with a ghost, and if we don't, he's going to drop the police on us? Is that right?"

Modesto stood and put out his hand. "Exactly. Welcome to the Hull family business."

Max buried his head on the desk. Sandra stared at Modesto

in shock. And Dr. Goldman made a quick exit.

"Well," Modesto said, dropping his unshaken hand. "I shall assume you'll consent to this arrangement unless I hear otherwise by the close of business today. Good day."

Max saluted with his hand and relished the perturbed huff he received in response. As Modesto exited, Sandra and Drummond closed in on the manila envelope. Max waved them off. He took the envelope and stuffed it in his top drawer. He didn't need to see Hull's specifics. The Hull family excelled at getting their way.

*For now,* Max thought. He had gotten the upper-hand on Hull once before; he could do it again.

The rest of the day dragged on. Drummond slipped away, and Sandra shuffled papers around in between bouts of alcohol-induced sleep. Max sat at his desk, trying to digest all that had happened.

As the business day neared its close, Sandra stepped in front of Max's desk wearing a stern, determined expression. "We need to talk," she said.

He pointed to his throat.

"Fine, I need to talk. You need to listen."

Max placed his hands behind his head, leaned back in his chair, and propped his feet on his desk. He smiled.

"Don't try to charm me. You listen. If we're going to be on retainer for Hull, and we both know we're going to be, then we've got to work out this whole working together thing for good. You seem to be struggling with the idea that your wife might be good at this."

Max shook his head, but Sandra put out her hand. "You don't get to argue this time. Ever since I started working here, you've acted out of sorts. You've been like another person towards me. I see you with Drummond or others and there's my Max, my honey, but whenever you have to deal with me, you become this other guy. I don't like that guy. Occasionally, you become you again and we have a great night and it seems like everything is okay. But then a day goes by and you're back to the Other Max.

"I don't know what's going on inside your head, but you need to figure it out. You need to remember that before we're business partners, and from now on we are business partners, but before that, we are married. We are husband and wife. And we love each other.

"I tried to work for you. That didn't do so well for either of us. So let's do this my way, instead. Let's just be a married couple. Let's just be in love. And let's let the fact that we work together not get between us. Do you think you can do that? Because I love you, and I don't want to lose you."

Max got to his feet and took Sandra's hands in his own. He closed his eyes as he brought her fingers to his lips. Leaning over the desk, he kissed her with a gentle touch.

"I can't hear you. Is that a yes?" she teased.

Max opened the top drawer of his desk, pulled out the manila envelope, and handed it to Sandra. "Yes," he said despite the pain.

Sandra pulled him close and pressed her lips hard against his. Locked in the embrace, Max never noticed Drummond's arrival until the ghost said, "If you two can stop the smooching, I got news."

Pushing Max back in his seat, Sandra said, "What is it?" She sat at her desk and opened the envelope.

Drummond watched her for a moment, clearly confused by the change in the office dynamic, but shrugged it off. "I thought you might like to know what became of Jasper Sullivan."

Both Max and Sandra perked up.

Drummond went on, "I put out the word that I was looking for him. The word came back to me. Nobody can find him. He's gone into hiding, maybe even found what he needed to move on. I'm not sure, but I can pretty much guarantee that we won't hear from him again."

"Is he that afraid of us?" Sandra asked. "What does he think we'll do to him?"

"You can't do much. But I can. And I would, too. Not only did he stiff us on getting paid, but the whole thing was a set-up for him. And I'll tell you one thing for sure — dead or alive, I do not like being set up."

"So he's running from you."

"I wish," Drummond said, clapping his hands and pointing at Max. "I think ol' Jasper is running more so from what Max did. By destroying the Corkilles, Max released all that energy back into the world, and dead energy released in a living world equals ghosts."

Sandra dug into the envelope as she said, "Jasper is running from the Corkilles."

"Wouldn't you?" Drummond said with a satisfied smile.

Sandra tossed the envelope onto Max's desk. "You ought to look in that."

Puzzled, Max reached in and pulled out their first check from the Hulls. He stared at it. His hands trembled. His stomach complained.

"If you won't deposit it," Sandra said, "I will."

Max looked up and handed her the check. She snatched it from him. Beckoning Drummond to tag along, she promised to be back soon.

Max turned to his computer, brought up the finance program, and entered the new income. It may not be palatable to work with Hull, but he promised himself it would only be temporary. Sandra was right about everything she had said. Together, he knew they could beat the Hulls.

Besides, as he watched that red number turn black, Max felt lighter. He didn't need to think twice about his next action. He hurried out of the office, rushed downstairs, and caught up with Sandra and Drummond on the sidewalk.

"Everything okay?" Sandra asked.

Max hooked his arm around her, kissed her cheek, and strolled toward the bank with a good friend on one side and the woman he loved on the other.

# Afterword

Regarding the history in *Southern Charm* - Korner's Folly is a real place and well worth a visit if you are ever near Kernersville, NC. If you don't live nearby, they have a website with photos so you can get a taste for what the place is like. Shortly before I had visited the house, a North Carolina paranormal society had indeed declared the building haunted (which just confirmed for me that it was perfect for this book).

Much of the true history of Blackbeard the Pirate is unknown which, for a writer, is license to create. So, as far as I know, Blackbeard never cavorted with a woman who used voodoo to curse him. It is true that no paintings of him exist and that he ran his operation (and finished his career in dramatic style) off the North Carolina coast, but all of his history with women was the result of my imagination.

As before, while many of the locations and histories are accurate, I do take liberties at times. Never forget - this is fiction.

# About the Author

Stuart Jaffe is the madman behind *The Max Porter Paranormal Mysteries,* the *Nathan K* thrillers, *The Parallel Society* series, *The Malja Chronicles, The Bluesman, Founders, Real Magic,* and so much more. His unique brand of old pulp adventure mixed with a contemporary sensibility brings out the best in a variety of SF/F sub-genres. He trained in martial arts for over a decade until a knee injury ended that practice. Now, he plays lead guitar in a local blues band, *The Bootleggers,* and enjoys life on a small farm in rural North Carolina. For those who continue to keep count, the animal list is as follows: one dog, two cats, three aquatic turtles, nine chickens, and a horse. As best as he's been able to manage, Stuart has made sure that the chickens and the horse do not live in the house.

*For more information, please visit www.stuartjaffe.com*

www.ingramcontent.com/pod-product-compliance
Lightning Source LLC
Chambersburg PA
CBHW030531310726
48979CB00010B/1875/J

* 9 7 8 1 7 3 3 7 3 0 8 4 6 *